THE MURDER AT THE MURDER AT THE MIMOSA INN

Joan Hess

St. Martin's Paperbacks

THE MURDER AT THE MURDER AT THE MIMOSA INN

Copyright © 1986 by Joan Hess.

Library of Congress Catalog Card Number: 86-13809

ISBN: 0-312-97178-8
EAN: 80312-97178-6

Printed in the United States of America

St. Martin's Paperbacks edition / October 1999

St. Martin's Paperbacks are published by St. Martin's Press, 175 Fifth Avenue, New York, NY 10010.

10 9 8 7 6 5 4 3

"THIS TIME, IT'S NO GAME."

I stared curiously at what I presumed was the bird-watchers' club. An icy finger danced up my spine as I took in their dazed expressions. A grebe could not be responsible for the strange stillness of the bird-watchers—no matter how peculiar its plumage, or idiosyncratic and public its mating habits.

After a whispered conversation with the woman, Peter came back to the croquet court to take Eric aside. The blood drained from Eric's face as he listened, and he began to sway with a queasy motion. The game halted, and mallets were slowly discarded. We formed a circle around Eric and Peter.

Peter took a deep breath. "Apparently the Audubon people hiked around the lake early this morning to a nesting area they explore on an annual basis. In one of the coves they found a rowboat, and in the rowboat a body—face down in several inches of water. There was a bloody indentation on the back of his head, and no doubt about his condition. I'm sorry to have to tell you that Harmon Crundall is dead. But this time, it's no game."

The Claire Malloy Mysteries
by Joan Hess

Strangled Prose

The Murder at the Murder at the Mimosa Inn

Dear Miss Demeanor

Roll Over and Play Dead

A Diet to Die For

A Really Cute Corpse

Death by the Light of the Moon

Poisoned Pins

A Holly, Jolly Murder

A Conventional Corpse

Out on a Limb

The Goodbye Body

Available from St. Martin's Paperbacks

For the ladies of the club, whose
friendship and support have meant everything to me:
Becky, Carolyn, Jane, Linda, Sara, and Terry

ONE

"Who's going to be murdered?"

"How should I know?"

"Then it's pure luck if you don't get stabbed in the back?"

"Of course not. The whole thing is arranged ahead of time. At the fateful moment, the designated victim keels over in the leeks or whatever."

"Well, what if it's you?" Peter continued with infuriating calmness. "You might end up in a coffin for the weekend, surrounded by flickering candles and funerary flower arrangements. It doesn't seem worth the price of admission."

I returned my attention to the last bite of filet on my plate, willing myself to remain unruffled despite a twinge of frustration. Until this moment, we had been chatting amiably about neutral topics, and I was beginning to admit to myself that I was attracted to the man. His opinions on the weather had coincided with my own, as had his views on used cars and the exorbitant price of hardback books. It took only one hint of mockery to undo the good work.

A waiter glided up to raise an eyebrow at the empty wine bottle. We all agreed that another bottle would be just the thing, and the waiter glided away to fetch it—and put it on the bill as well as the table.

"I will not be a victim," I said, resolved to be patient, if not charitable. "As you have pointed out so astutely, I am paying for the pleasure of solving a murder. I intend to be quite superior at it."

"Since you've had so much experience . . . ?"

Peter, known to his colleagues as Lieutenant Rosen of the Farbeville CID, flashed his teeth at me. We had been introduced over a corpse; there had been a bit of competition during the subsequent investigation. I had been accused of meddling. Interfering. Sticking my graceful nose into danger. Disrupting the investigation. All of that was unjust; my contribution had been invaluable—and unacknowledged. It had also led to the dinner date with Peter Rosen, although I wasn't at all sure I had been wise to accept.

He was a handsome man, in an arrogant, New Yorkish way. Curly black hair with a few gray notes, a jutting beak and deceptively mild, molasses-colored eyes. His taste in clothing was impeccable and expensive, with an emphasis on the three-piece look. Divorced, which was convenient for those of us who preferred uncomplicated relationships—if there was a relationship in the making. I certainly didn't know. However, I was willing to find out, as long as there was a free meal included in the deal, and a bottle or two of lovely red wine.

I am a mild-mannered bookseller, blessed with wit and red hair. I am widowed, self-sufficient, and a reasonably competent parent of my fourteen-year-old daughter, Caron. Those who have such a creature in the house will quickly grasp the ramifications of the age; those who do not will never believe the horror stories, so I shall subside on the topic. It will, regrettably, resurface later.

"When and where is the murder to take place?" Peter asked.

"This weekend at the Mimosa Inn, about twenty miles west of town. It used to be a retreat for some Texas oilman; now it's owned by one of Carlton's old students, Eric Vanderhan. I fed the boy spaghetti for almost four years and allowed him to babysit so that I could attend feminist lectures on the evils of motherhood. I'm going as a favor to him and his wife."

"Oh, I see," Peter murmured, nodding wisely. "As long as you're not going out of some fanciful desire to play Miss Marple, it makes perfectly good sense."

"I am going to play Miss Marple." I managed a smile, although it took some effort. "We've been asked to wear costumes for high tea Friday afternoon."

"Beside the croquet court, no doubt."

My lips began to ache, but did not fail me. "Actually, yes. Everyone is going to dress as his or her favorite detective from mystery fiction. It will enhance the ambiance of the weekend."

"Enhance the ambiance?" He was trying not to laugh, but with no great success. Teeth glinted like blunted icicles. "I can picture you skulking down some dark corridor in your orthopedic shoes, a knitting needle clutched in your hand. The murderer steps out of the shadows! A muffled scream, the lights go out—and then, a puddle of blood seeps under the door. Murder most foul!"

The waiter had reappeared in the middle of Peter's ravings. From the guarded expression on his face, I suspected he had overheard the last few words. The wine bottle was opened with undue briskness, and the waiter left for the kitchen to relate the story to the dishwasher. A slow evening, rescued by the crazies in the last booth.

"I don't find it all that amusing," I said. My patience was ebbing, as was my resolution to maintain it, and my lips were protesting like college students in the late sixties.

"Murder weekends are fashionable on both coasts. They're staged on cruises, on trains and in penthouses as an exercise in deduction and quickwitted observation. I have no idea how it will be presented, but I think it will be fun—and I fully intend to win the case of champagne."

Peter picked up his glass and swirled the wine to capture the candlelight. "The idea of adults behaving like ghoulish bloodhounds leaves me cold, Claire. Murder is not a comedy—it's a tragedy, not only for the victim but also for the murderer and those around him."

He was right, of course. I had learned that he often was, much to my chagrin, but I wasn't going to admit it. Honor before honesty.

"Your perspective is different, Peter. You deal with the reality of violence. This is a game, and everyone knows it from the beginning. The whole thing is plotted very carefully; the actors have the situation under control at all times. No one really gets hurt or does any tortured soul-searching. It's a spectator sport, and it's no more brutal than watching a boxing match or a football game."

"I suppose not," he said, "as long as everyone knows the rules of the game. . . ."

"Don't be silly." I laughed. "It's only a game."

"It's a silly, mindless, juvenile game!" Caron huffed, her nostrils aquiver with postpubescent indignation. "I am not about to waste a weekend in some remote shanty, creeping around on my hands and knees to hunt for fingerprints in the grass! I'd have to jump-start my brain when it was over!"

"It's actually a very trendy thing to do, Caron," I said with sympathy and understanding, privately noting what a drain the weekend plans were beginning to put on my more admirable virtues. "All of your friends will be envious when you tell them about it."

"There's a rock concert Saturday night at the college

gymnasium, Mother. Inez and I were planning to go, and—"

"You're going to the Mimosa Inn," I countered, giving her the famed maternal eye. It was supposed to cut off the argument, squelch the pleas, end the futile bargaining.

"But, Mother," Caron continued in a whine that could shatter crystal at fifty feet, "why do I have to go? I could stay here by myself, and keep the Book Depot open for you. Inez can spend the night Saturday after the concert."

"That is what terrifies me. You and Inez are capable of disaster, and the idea of turning you two loose on Farberville is irresponsible, inhumane, and possibly felonious."

I made a cup of tea and started for my bedroom, while visions of the San Francisco earthquake danced in my head. "There will be no further discussion, Caron," I added firmly. "We have a double room at the Mimosa Inn, which is in no way a 'remote shanty.' It is a luxurious country inn, with swimming and boating and all sorts of activities. You can spend two days fishing, if you wish, or participate in the murder, but you'll undoubtedly have a lovely time."

"Fishing?" she squealed. "I'm supposed to fish?" She seemed to equate it with a root canal or amputation. Sans anesthesia.

Motherhood wasn't at all what it was purported to be. I took refuge in my bedroom. As I closed the door, I heard a faint hiss of disgust drifting from the living room. The word "Worms!" punctuated the sound.

We left Farberville late Friday morning. The highway curled through a broad valley carpeted with green shag. Laconic cows munched daisies, colts dashed across pastures, hawks effortlessly spiraled in the sky. Very bucolic, I thought, ignoring the occasional sigh from the passenger's side. Caron would survive the ordeal, and a brief respite from Inez would give both of us a chance to reestablish our relationship. Inez is a sweet girl, but she tends to reinforce

Caron's melodramatic side. I was convinced I had made the
right decision, although the oxygen inside the car was being
depleted at an alarming rate.

"There's the sign," I said cheerfully. "The Mimosa Inn
is about four miles from the highway, so we ought to be
there in time for lunch. Are you hungry?"

"I'm on a diet, Mother. I don't eat lunch."

I toyed with a lecture on the perils of anorexia, but left it
for another time. "Well, I'm famished. The food is reputed
to be excellent."

"It's probably fish. I don't see why ingesting fish is
supposed to increase your intelligence, since they are
probably the very stupidest of all the craniate vertebrates!
They eat worms, you know."

I tightened my grip on the steering wheel and turned
down the gravel road. A lovely weekend, I told myself in a
controlled voice. No squabbles, no lectures. An opportunity
to explore my daughter's mind, to open the channels of
communication à la Spock. On the other hand, if a second
victim was needed, a candidate came to mind.

We bounced along in silence. The road wound around a
low mountain and past a sorry farmhouse surrounded by
bleached outbuildings held upright by barbed wire, splin-
tery boards, and a goodly amount of prayer. Caron made a
gurgling noise as she stared out the window. An obscenely
enormous hog had discovered nirvana in several inches of
greenish mud. No comment was forthcoming, but I wondered if pork chops had just been eliminated from the diet,
along with lunch.

Pastures were replaced with woods filled with oaks and
scrub pines. It did not qualify as a primeval forest, only a
stunted tangle of unpretentious brush and moldering leaves.
Although Farberville was just a few miles away, we were in
the wilderness. I do not particularly relish the outdoor life—
mosquitos and poison ivy having an affinity for my flesh—
but I was determined to make an effort.

We stopped at a wrought-iron gate spanning a cattle

guard. The paint on the gate had peeled, but the sign hanging from it was fresh and encouraging: WELCOME TO THE MIMOSA INN.

"Excited?" I asked Caron.

"Thrilled to death," she sighed. "Fish. Worms. A bunch of old people playing games. Costume parties and croquet, for pity's sake! You don't even like champagne, Mother. You never drink it. Why do we have to come all the way out here just to—"

"I like the idea of champagne," I interrupted briskly, "and it will be fun, Caron, if you'll give it a chance. This is an exercise in mental agility, in abstract reasoning and problem solving. Why, this may prove to be more valuable than your geometry class."

"And just as much fun."

I glanced at her. She had almost disappeared into the vinyl upholstery of the seat. Her lower lip was extended in a mute display of petulance, but she had enough sense not to continue the remarks. She was probably counting the minutes under her breath and reminding herself that this, too, would pass.

A large lake appeared on our right. Surrounded by low mountains, it lacked the grandeur of Superior but looked adequate for sailing and swimming. Seconds later we saw the inn. I braked abruptly as my eyes widened.

"It looks like a wedding cake," Caron whispered, jolted out of her sulk by the sight. "All it needs is a pair of oversized mannequins on the turret and a ring of pink sugar roses. Are we really supposed to stay there?"

Caron's description was accurate. The Mimosa Inn was a three-story Victorian house slathered with gingerbread trim, curlicues, round windows with stained glass, turrets, weather vanes, and almost everything else one could attach to a structure without toppling it. The front of the house faced the lake over a broad expanse of lawn, and on the porch we could see large wicker chairs and potted plants. A gray wedding cake, trimmed in white, I amended silently, glad we had not arrived on a foggy day, or a dark and stormy night.

"Yes, we are," I said when I could trust my voice. As long as I didn't have to climb any spiral staircases to track down clues, or explore the cellar for pertinent cobwebs amidst the unmarked graves. I don't do cobwebs.

"Is it haunted?" Caron gulped.

"Do you believe in ghosts?"

Caron finally gained control of her dangling jaw. "No, I don't, Mother. I feel that inexplicable psi phenomena usually have a basis in paraphysical energy sources. We did a chapter on it in physics last semester. It was very informative."

She rambled on in that vein as we drove around the house to a parking area under a clump of trees. An erstwhile stable now housed cars; inside was a daunting array of Mercedes, Cadillacs, etc. My dented Japanese hatchback would prefer fresh air, I told myself as I cut off the engine. The stillness was sudden, complete. And a tad unsettling for those of us who spend our days on a busy street and our nights next to a college campus. Ah, nature at its quietest . . .

While we were struggling with our suitcases (Caron's three and my overnight bag), a blond man opened the door. His extreme height and rambling gait gave him a disjointed look, as though he were a marionette controlled by a clumsy puppet-master. His wire-rimmed glasses had gray adhesive-tape cocoons at each corner, and his shirt pocket sagged under the weight of his pen collection. White socks and torn sneakers. I reminded myself that this man had written a nationally acclaimed textbook on an aspect of higher mathematics that I could not pronounce.

He grinned and flapped a hand in welcome. "Claire! I've been watching the road for you. I'm so glad that you finally came; it's going to be a splendid weekend."

"Hello, Eric," I puffed, disengaging Caron's garment

bag from the back seat. I introduced him to Caron, who managed a muttered response to his enthusiastic greeting.

"And how are you, Claire?" He covered me with a hug. "I was so sorry to hear about Dr. Malloy's accident. He was a great teacher and a good friend."

But not a careful driver, I added to myself. "Thanks, Eric. I was astounded to hear you were back in the area. What on earth possessed you to buy and renovate a country inn? You were always the outdoor type, as in ivy towers and cramped offices."

"Wait until you meet my wife," he said. His face glowed as if he were a child on Christmas morning. "She's a city girl, and she's always wanted to escape to the country. Cows and chickens, that sort of thing. We saw an ad for the place. Two months later we signed the papers."

I looked up at a copper rooster rotating in the breeze. "So you gave up your faculty position—and tenure—to come here?"

"We did. The royalties from the book paid for the remodeling and furnishings. Once we start the publicity, we hope that the Mimosa Inn can pay for itself. Until then, we'll have to struggle along. I'm so glad you're here, Claire. Let's get you and Caron checked in."

I found his narrative hard to believe. Eric was as much a naturalist as I; neither of us could survive in a city park for more than an hour. I was curious to meet the woman who had lured him away from the relative safety of academia.

"So what do you think of the setting?" he said as we shuffled up a brick sidewalk with enough luggage to take a six-week safari into the remotest jungle—*and* dress for dinner every night.

"The house is magnificent," I said. "The lake is beautiful, the woods woody, the sky unsullied by carbon monoxide. The one thing I don't see is an orchard of mimosa trees."

"The inn is named after my wife."

"Your wife's name is Mimosa?" I twittered. Politely, I hoped.

Eric peered down at me. "Mimi. But we are going to plant mimosa trees as soon as we can afford them."

We did a Three Stooges routine in the doorway. After a round of grunts and embarrassed laughs, Caron popped out and skittered into a large open room. I followed with more dignity, gazing around at the high ceiling and antiques that rather overpowered the room.

A small desk sat near the entrance, and behind it a closed door with a discreet sign that suggested it was private, though no threat followed. The furnishings were straight out of a period English novel, from the brocade to the chintz, from the sheers to the brass knickknacks cluttering mahogany surfaces. An aroma of lemon oil competed with more prosaic variety from the lake. It all gleamed and glittered. Only the butler was missing, and I wasn't sure where we could put him.

"My goodness," I managed to murmur, trying to sound awed rather than shell-shocked. "How charming."

"Do you like it? Mimi felt that we ought to try for a sense of subdued gentility. Luckily, an elderly aunt died at the right time, leaving an attic crammed with furniture." He gave us a bemused smile. "Luckily for us, anyway. Aunt Beatrice may have felt differently."

Caron opened her mouth to offer an editorial on the interior decorator—or on Aunt Beatrice's postmortem generosity. I stepped in front of her and said, "I'm looking forward to meeting Mimi, Eric."

"She's excited about finally meeting you. However, just now she's rushing around upstairs to see about bedrooms and towels and such, so you'll have to wait until things are settled."

Eric let the luggage thump to the floor, took out a large leather book, and showed me where to sign it. With an antique fountain pen, naturally. I would have done Caron's name in crayon, considering her attitude, but that would have destroyed the charming appearance of the registration book. Ambiance.

We then regathered the luggage and staggered up a long flight of stairs to the second floor. To my relief, Aunt Beatrice's furniture had only been inadequate for the main floor; the bedroom was simply furnished but comfortable. An antique bed and dresser, and a dressing table with a calico skirt, all sitting on a braided rug. I forgave Eric the ceramic pitcher and bowl, on the assumption that it was only for display, and found a closet and a modern bathroom. Caron found the bed.

"I'm eager to meet Mimi," I told Eric, "but I'm eager to solve a murder, too. Tell me what happens now."

He took a folded brochure from the top of the dresser and handed it to me. "Here's the schedule for the weekend, Claire. There's a salad buffet in the dining room, and you'll want to explore the grounds before the lecture begins at two o'clock."

"Lecture?" Caron groaned, fluttering her eyelashes from the depths of a pillow.

Eric was clearly unacquainted with adolescent tragedy. He squinted at her as though she were some elusive logarithm, then said, "It's optional, of course. If you'd prefer, you can sail one of the little boats or swim. I'm afraid there aren't any young people to entertain you. The group is on the older side, except for your eternally youthful mother."

Caron forced one eye open. "Where's the pool?"

"We don't have a pool," Eric answered warily. He was intelligent enough to see what was coming, but too inexperienced to do much about it. He and his wife were childless, obviously. After two days with Caron, they would gladly sign an oath to maintain their status quo.

I tried to intercept the missile. "You'll swim in the lake, Caron. I know this will come as a shock, but swimming pools did not play a vital role in the American way of life until the last decade. People were actually forced to swim in lakes, rivers, and even the ocean."

The other eye was turned on me. "With fish?"

Eric cleared his throat as the missile continued on its course. "The lake is stocked, but only with bass and catfish. No barracuda or sharks or anything like that."

"But the fish stay in the water all the time. That means that they do all sorts of gross things right where a person is supposed to swim. I'd rather eat spiders." The missile having razed its intended target, Caron pulled the pillow over her head. A series of uncooperative noises ensued.

I shrugged at Eric and motioned for him to join me in the hallway. We walked downstairs to what I now mentally deemed the drawing room. "So you've had the inn less than a year? Have you had many guests?"

"This is our busiest weekend thus far. There are only about twenty guests, and it's quite a mixed group. But everyone is a mystery fan." He led me across the drawing room to a pair of curtained French doors. "Here's the dining room, Claire. Have a bit of lunch, although I must warn you that we're pushing sherry for the weekend. Mimi thinks it's appropriate, considering the scenario."

I was not feeling terribly kindly toward the unseen Mimi, since I lump sherry in the same category that Caron does piscatory bodily productions. However, I managed a civilized tone. "I'll read the schedule while I eat, Eric, but tell me what to expect. Will a troupe of actors produce the murder on stage after dinner?"

He waggled a finger at me. "Now, that wouldn't be fair. You'll just have to wait and see what develops. The murderer could sit beside you during dinner or creep up behind you in the hallway. But from what I've heard about your detecting prowess, this ought to be a piece of cake."

"Oh?" I said, displeased by the thought that certain past events were the topic of conversation on Farberville street corners. "If you'll excuse me, I'll do my homework while I eat lunch. Will you be at the lecture?"

The finger waggled again. "That would be telling, wouldn't it?"

Sighing, I went into the dining room and studied my cohorts for the murder weekend. Most of them had already eaten, I brilliantly deduced as I filled a plate and sat down at a corner table. Two elderly couples glanced at me but continued to whisper across the table to each other. A white-haired woman with a long, equine face was the only other diner. She gave me a frosty smile over a forkful of shrimp, which regained her attention before I could reciprocate.

The sixth person in the room was a thirtyish man with oiled black hair and a thin moustache, who was looking out the window. Very suspicious. I determined to remain alert and cautious. The murderer might be anyone, although the elderly couples appeared superficially harmless. In fact, I was garnering quite a few quick peeks from their table, as if they suspected me of potential mayhem. Me, for God's sake. I shot them a haughty look over my artichoke heart.

A pimply busboy in a starched white coat asked me what I would prefer to drink. He looked too naive to hear the truth, so I requested iced tea and settled back to read the brochure.

"You Are Invited to a Murder," the opening line informed me slyly from a circle of whimsical red splotches. It went on:

Friday

12:00   Luncheon

2:00   Lecture by Sergeant Nicholas Merrick of Scotland Yard

5:00   Tea/sherry on the veranda: Famous Literary Detectives

8:00   Dinner

10:00   Movie: *Murder on the Orient Express*

Saturday

9:00   Breakfast
1:00   Luncheon
2:00   Croquet tournament
5:00   Tea/sherry on the veranda
8:00   Dinner
9:00   Gala champagne party and presentation of sleuthing awards

Sunday

10:00   Brunch
11:00   Checkout

I read it carefully several times for clues or hints, of which there were none. The two couples and the elderly lady drifted out of the dining room, all studiously avoiding my veiled scrutiny. The competition did not look keen, I concluded. A piece of cake, as Eric had assumed earlier—and a case of champagne to show Peter Rosen who was the abler detective. I brooded for a minute, amazed by the competitive drive that sprang from the mere mention of his name. Surely I was there for the mental challenge, the stimulating puzzle, the love of mystery fiction—wasn't I?

"Phooey on him!" I hissed under my breath.

The oily-haired man looked up at the comment. He gave me a broad smile, which I interpreted as an invitation for conversation. My first suspect, falling into my artichoke hearts. The game was afoot.

"Why don't you join me for coffee?" I cooed.

"Thank you, I'd enjoy that." He carried a cup and saucer to my table and sat down across from me. He had a round boyish face and a slight paunch, as if middle age had crept up on him while he was engaged in sedentary pursuits. A plaid sports coat did nothing to enhance his shape. But a suspect is a suspect.

He demolished my hopes with his first sentence. "I'm Nicholas Merrick."

"From Scotland Yard? The detective who's giving the lecture at two o'clock? You were my very first suspect for the murder, but you won't do—although you don't sound very English. Claire Malloy," I added with a desultory attempt at decorum. We shook hands across the table.

"I hope that I sound like a pharmaceutical sales representative from Farberville, since that's what I am. Scotland Yard turned down our request, so I agreed to take the role. My accent doesn't ring true, but my heart is pure. What about you?"

I told him about the Book Depot and my secret fantasy to outsleuth Miss Marple (and unspecified policemen) and win the champagne. He made a few comments about mystery fiction, but carefully avoided anything about the murder that was to occur. I tried a few studiously casual questions, and received only evasions in return. Phooey.

Nickie, as I discovered he preferred, looked at his watch and stood up. "It's almost one now, and I need to see if the slide projector is ready. Will you attend the lecture?"

We walked to the drawing room together. "I certainly will. My daughter is with me, however, and I'd better look in on her before it begins. She may have tied the sheets together in order to climb out the window and bolt for civilization."

"Is she locked in the room?" Nickie asked, eyeing me with a sudden coolness.

"No," I sighed. "The problem is that the door's too easy. I'll see you in an hour, Nickie." I started for the stairs.

"Claire?"

I turned around. "Yes?"

"Why did you glower earlier and mutter a virulent 'phooey' in my direction?"

"I was thinking of someone else," I admitted with a

laugh. "I never phooey strangers, unless I suspect them of vile crimes."

"But now your suspicions are allayed?"

I was in no mood to go into my weekend strategy, so I settled for a conspiratorial wink and said, "I'll trust no one until the murderer is unmasked. A criminal in every corner."

The man from Scotland Yard looked at me with a curiously blank expression. His fingers found the tip of his moustache as his eyes went blink, blink, blink.

T W O

Caron had not moved while I was downstairs. Motivated by a vague motherly obligation, I ascertained from a prudent distance that she was breathing, then began to drag suitcases around the room. All this elicited a single sniffle. I unpacked my overnight case, hung a severe black dress complete with lace collar in the closet alongside a sensible cardigan sweater, arranged the orthopedic shoes under it, and took a small spiral notebook from my purse.

"I'm going back down for the lecture," I announced politely. After receiving a sniffle in response, I eased the door closed and went downstairs. It was not yet one-thirty. I opted to reconnoiter the scene of the crime so that I would be equipped with a mental map when the crucial moment arrived. The scouts and I would be prepared.

The croquet court was a recent addition to the landscape. It consisted of a large rolled surface edged with boards buried in the turf. The wickets conformed to whatever arrangement was demanded by the rules, about which I had no theories. A cart with mallets and balls had been wheeled near one corner, but no one had availed himself of the equipment. Nor did I; I was on a mission.

I strolled down the slope to the edge of the lake. Several bodies lay on beach towels in the grass, but none of them looked like victims of anything more dire than incipient sunburn. A few heads lifted, a few eyes studied me from the safety of dark lenses. Which one was the murderer? I decided that a plump woman in a bikini deserved some form of painful death for exposing white, undulating ripples of fat, but left that mean-spirited conclusion unspoken.

A boathouse sat at the edge of the cove, surrounded by a minor armada of sailboats and rowboats. I continued past it to follow a graveled path through a rose garden. In the middle I found a stained marble statue of a chubby urchin with a pitcher on his shoulder. It had been a long time since any water had dribbled down his tummy, but the effect had potential.

As I came out of the garden, I saw three shingled bungalows in a line, separated by shrubs. Shutters were fastened across the windows. They were used only during the busy season, I deduced brilliantly. I stopped in front of the first one and cupped my hands on the pane of glass in the door. I ended up with a circle of dirt on my nose. The interior of the bungalow was, quite naturally, dark.

"Very suspicious," I murmured aloud, savoring the feel of the words. They would be my motto for the weekend, my watchword whenever approached by anything or anyone even remotely inexplicable. Champagne had the same effect on my nose as ragweed, but I *did* like the idea of it. Festive, triumphant champagne. It was unfortunate that scotch did not carry the same connotation; it certainly was more agreeable to drink.

It was nearing lecture time. I followed the path back to the boathouse, where I discovered that the bodies on the beach had vanished. "Very suspicious," I practiced as I went to the porch, "very, very suspicious."

The ladderback chairs from the dining room had been brought to the drawing room and arranged in rows. Eric waved from a corner, intent on a slide projector. Nickie Merrick stood behind a podium at the front of the room, his expression somewhat pinched as he faced a group of twenty or so people vying for the more comfortable chairs.

Overachiever that I have been since the first day of nursery school, I took a seat in the middle of the front row and smiled at Nickie. "Stage fright?"

"No, I've done quite a bit of acting." He stared over my head, absently tugging at his mustache. "A minor problem has arisen, I'm afraid. Mimi's more than capable of dealing with it, but she was hoping that things would go smoothly. Now it seems that—"

"Sherry?" brayed an incredulous voice from the dining room. "Sherry is for puppeteers and little old ladies with blue hair! Bring me a bottle of scotch, sonny boy!"

A plate crashed on the floor.

"Now, you feeble-minded, pimple-nosed excuse for a human being! Now!" the voice continued. It sounded as though it were being amplified by a bullhorn, static and all. A second plate hit the floor. Several other voices joined in, none of them jolly.

All of us turned around to stare at the interior of the dining room. Eric, I noted out of the corner of my eye, had frozen in the act of fiddling with a knob; his mouth was white and his fingers curled like talons. Gradually, his hand relaxed, but his frown did not. The pipe between his teeth was in danger of bisection.

The busboy scurried around the corner and ducked into the office. Seconds later, a tulip-shaped glass sailed out in a graceful arch. We held our collective breath as it splattered on the floor, shards of glass erupting in glittery explosion. The tinkle was as loud as a grenade in the shocked hugh.

"Damn it," Nickie said quietly behind me. He hurried over to Eric for a terse conference. As they started for the dining room, a woman came out of the room and closed the door behind her. The three exchanged looks, then the woman pasted on a smile and came forward.

"Please don't worry about—about that minor incident," she said coolly. "An unexpected guest has arrived, and he wasn't prepared for our little game. But it's under control now, and the lecture will begin any minute."

I studied the woman, who I realized was the heretofore unseen Mimi. She had shoulder-length black hair, wide violet eyes, and cheekbones high enough to give her a vaguely exotic look. Her mouth was small and heart-shaped, as though she were sweetly pouting. Although she could have passed for a college student, there were a few fine lines around her eyes, and her forehead, at the moment, was scored by two deep creases. A certain softness under her chin also belied the little-girl picture. I am personally familiar with that symptom.

Mimi kept the determined smile on her face as she nudged Nickie toward the front of the room. "Please don't be concerned," she added with a shrug. "The gentleman in question will soon be plied with scotch. Everything is fine."

Despite unconvinced looks from all present, she held her ground. The busboy rushed back into the dining room with an amber bottle clutched in his hand. A rumble of approval was followed by a tantalizing clink of glass. I caught myself wondering if I ought to try the same barbaric tactics and gave myself a mental scolding. I would drink sherry—and like it. Ambiance over self-indulgence.

Nickie tapped the podium with a pencil. With the ingrained obedience of a Sunday school class, we turned around and assumed attentive expressions. Behind me I heard a shuffle of feet and final coughs. The white-haired horsy woman sat down beside me and gave me a vague smile. Very suspicious, I cautioned myself, although I had no idea why the gesture might be suspicious.

"Welcome to the first 'Murder at the Mimosa Inn,' "

Nickie said. "We're delighted to have you join us, and we're going to do our very best to amuse and entertain you." He took out a brochure to run over the schedule, then described the various facilities available for those who opted not to worry about the impending crime.

Keeping my eyes straight ahead, I nudged the woman beside me and whispered out of the corner of my mouth, "Who's the loud-mouthed oaf in the dining room?"

In response, I received a painful elbow in the ribs and a priggish, disgusted snort. Clearly, my neighbor was not the sort who whispered in church or tolerated such childishness. I decided not to engage in a game of elbowing; the woman had a vastly sharper weapon than I.

Nickie finished the schedule and put the brochure away. "Part of the fun is not knowing when or how the murder will take place," he warned us genially. "Be prepared for anything, including a few bloopers on our part. The Mimosa Inn and the Farberville Community Theater are both novices at this newest sport, and anything can happen. Keep your eyes open and your back to the wall."

The woman next to me lifted an alabaster finger. "Could the murderer be one of the guests?" she asked in a melodious voice that didn't fool me one bit. I knew to whom she referred, the silly old thing. And her hair wasn't white; it was blue. And thin.

Nickie shook his head. "I'm afraid I can't answer that, Mrs.—ah . . . ?"

"Mrs. Robison-Dewitt," the treacherous woman said, inching away from me. "I'm the editor of the *Ozark Chronicle*. We've scheduled an article on the murder weekend for our autumn edition." She paused to give the rest of us a chance to gasp in admiration, then said, "I presume that our personal safety is assured?"

She sounded as though she were anticipating a crazed attack from the innocent party on her left. If I had stashed a water gun in my purse, I would have doused her on the spot to watch her melt. I was obliged to settle for a well-bred sniff.

Nickie looked at me and grinned. "Your personal safety is assured, Mrs. Robison-Dewitt. Trust me. Now, if your questions have been answered, I'd like to begin the lecture. Since we know why we're here, I thought you might enjoy hearing how Scotland Yard utilizes various technological advances to solve its very real crimes."

He gestured at Eric, who was back at his post beside the projector. The lights went out and the screen behind Nickie lit up with a view of New Scotland Yard. Mrs. Robison-Dewitt stiffened, but gradually relaxed as nothing dreadful happened to impinge on her personal safety, meaning that I didn't leap on her. I crossed my legs, settled back, and listened intently.

Nickie was good, I decided, as he talked knowledgeably about his subject. I was aware of a certain amount of restiveness behind me, but I found the lecture informative and enjoyable. As he talked, he fielded questions and allowed a certain amount of diversion from his topic. We were all eager for help, although we lacked polygraphs, saliva kits, and other such paraphernalia.

He had just introduced the use of psychology to analyse sociopathic personalities, when a voice from the back of the room interrupted. My composure went the way of the tulip glass.

"Does a psychologist have a chance with a truly insane mind?" The tone was properly sincere, but the hint of mockery was unavoidable. The voice belonged to the one person who was not supposed to be within twenty miles of the Mimosa Inn. The one person who had scoffed at my weekend plans and expressed amusement at the whole concept.

"Damn!" I hissed like a pressure cooker on the verge of explosion, which was a pertinent analogy.

"Do you mind . . . ?" Mrs. Robinson-Dewitt hissed in response.

I minded, but there wasn't any point in including the woman in my decidedly black thoughts. What was he doing there? Peter Rosen had scoffed—and laughed—at the idea; why had he come? I swiveled my head to find him in the back of the room, wishing grimly that I would discover that I was mistaken, that he hadn't really asked the skeptical question. I saw silhouettes, but I couldn't spot him in the rows of people.

While all this was going on, Nickie Merrick was answering the question in a serious manner. The damned voice goaded him on, then suddenly switched positions and began a barrage of medical questions about schizophrenic chemical deficiencies. It was much too complex to bother with; I focused all my energy on holding in a series of semihysterical comments about unwanted people popping up at inopportune moments to destroy otherwise perfectly pleasant plans.

Nickie finally admitted defeat and turned on the lights. "Our speaker in the back of the room seems better acquainted with this material than I, so perhaps you might continue this with him if you're interested." He was not as pleased as he tried to sound, but it was a graceful escape.

We all blinked in the sudden flush of light. Chairs creaked and possessions were shuffled as the group began to rise. Eric stepped to the podium and said, "As you have heard, there will be a croquet tournament tomorrow afternoon. The winners will receive silver trays with a suitable engraved motif. If you're unfamiliar with the game, I'll be delighted to offer instruction this afternoon. In the meantime, enjoy the facilities at the Inn. Swim, nap in the sun, or allow Mimi to arrange a bridge game on the porch. However, those who search may find a clue to the identity of the murderer."

Mrs. Robison-Dewitt rose, looked down her nose at me, and forced her way through the crowd with the tact of a metallic gray battleship. I sat. Eric Vanderhan was engulfed in a circle of would-be sleuths, who demanded further explanations of his casual comment about clues. Nickie Merrick gave me a quick salute and left the room. I methodically crossed every toe and finger and made a wish that wasn't the least bit polite. It didn't work.

"Claire," Peter said as he sat down in the chair beside me, "are you enjoying the weekend thus far?"

"Up until just a few minutes ago, I was having a lovely time," I said sweetly. "But I'm surprised to see you. Surprised is, in truth, an understatement. What are you doing here?" I received a view of his teeth and a shrug. "What are you doing here?" I repeated in a voice edged with frost. Mrs. Robison-Dewitt could not have done better, although she had had more practice as an iceberg.

"Well," he said, "it sounded like great fun, so I decided to come at the last minute. I was fortunate to find a room, don't you think?"

"Astoundingly fortunate," I agreed drily.

"And I was pining away for a glimpse of your angelic face and emerald green eyes. When I could no longer bear the misery, I threw a suitcase in the trunk and raced down the highway."

I toyed with a maidenly blush, but opted for a raised eyebrow and a little-bitty frown of irritation. Angelic face and emerald eyes, indeed! "If you're quite finished spouting nonsense, I'd like to know the real reason why you came to the Mimosa Inn, Peter. You made your position clear at the restaurant—"

"Did I? I wasn't at all sure that I did."

The enigmatic response caught me unprepared. I stopped for a minute to ponder his obscure reference, then dismissed it as drivel, which it was. Nothing had happened at the restaurant, or afterward. I gritted my teeth and once again said, "Why are you here? If you don't explain, I'm going to fetch the knitting needle from my room and we'll test your nasty little scenario about murder in the hall. We need a victim, and you'd be so good at lying in state." He certainly was adept at lying in his teeth.

"I appreciate your confidence in me, but you'll have to accept my explanation, Claire. Would you like to join me on the porch for a cup of tea?"

"No, I would not." My little-bitty frown grew a little-bitty bit darker. "Why don't you admit that you came because you couldn't bear the idea of my winning the game and proving myself a better detective? I fear your ego is showing."

"I believe you're worried about the competition," he said, feigning astonishment and then concern. "If that is the case, I'll be happy to stand aside and allow you to win."

"Thank you so very much. In the meantime, you can take your magnifying glass and fingerprint kit and—and stuff it in your teacup!"

I snatched up my notebook and stalked out of the room. Once on the porch, I looked around wildly for a destination that would take me a long way from Peter. Walking across the lake was out, even in my martyred state of mind. I had already explored the path beside the boathouse and the garden beyond. I started down the steps, changed my mind, and went back to a wicker chair, where I flopped down. The chair creaked in protest of the brutal treatment.

"Why, lookee here, Suzetta, a real live detective," said a voice behind me. "Found any bodies, honey?"

. I clamped down on my lip until my initial response faded, then turned around to study the two people sitting at a small round table. A bottle of scotch (my brand) sat in the middle of the table; a good half of it was gone. From the slightly unfocused eyes beaming at me, I could deduce where it was.

The man appeared to be past middle-aged prime, and his life-style had contributed to the decline. A polyester jacket failed to span a protruding belly. Sparse white hair was combed in an improbable path across his pink scalp, which paled in comparison to the noticeably red nose below. Shaggy white eyebrows, a roadmap of wrinkles on mottled skin, and two wet lips, continually and unnecessarily moistened by a flickering tongue, completed the distasteful picture.

His companion was a contrast in every sense. She—very definitely she—had ash blond hair that artlessly cascaded down her shoulders. Cornflower blue eyes ringed by heavy lashes, a generous mouth outlined in scarlet, a body that could have paraded down the Atlantic City runway without a moment of hesitation. She wore a scarlet halter that covered everything absolutely illegal to display in public, but not an inch more than that. Long, tanned legs originated from brief white shorts; her toenails matched her lipstick.

All in all, neither was my type. The scotch, however, was. Feigning a smile, I said, "Then you're not here for the murder weekend?"

"Hell, no, sweetie pie! Suzetta and I came down here for a nice quiet time together." A leer to emphasize the fact that he wasn't talking about croquet or bass fishing. "Didn't we, Suzetta baby?"

Suzetta batted her spider-leg lashes at him. "No, we sure were surprised, weren't we, Harmon? But I think it's kinda cute, in a spooky way. I'll bet my honey bear could find out who the mean old murderer was before any of these people."

"I sure could, honey bunch." He patted her hand, then gave me a big wink. "But then I wouldn't have time to take care of my doll and make sure she has a good time here in the wild. Wild—get it?"

The man was on the verge of an oink, I told myself in a cold voice. I abhor the type, and had trustingly presumed they had gone the way of the dinosaurs. No such luck. I gave the bottle of scotch an envious look and stood up.

"Lovely chatting with you," I said.

"Don't you want to stay and have a little snort with us?" Harmon said, patting the chair beside him. I could almost feel his pudgy fingers on my anatomy. Pride battled with Johnny Walker.

I sat down in the indicated chair and bobbled my head politely. "Well, perhaps a small drink. I'm not particularly fond of sherry, and neither are you, from what I heard earlier."

"Horse piss," Harmon agreed generously. He bellowed at the hovering busboy to bring another glass, then ran his eyes over my body. I had never felt it to be inferior, but Harmon seemed to prefer Suzetta's voluptuous lines. I am sleek—less wind resistance.

Suzetta pursed her lips. "You must be real brave to want to creep around this old house with a murderer. Why, I don't know what I'd do if someone was after me. I'm such a 'fraidy cat that I'd probably just faint if someone touched me." She produced a girlish shiver, which elicited a paternal moan from Harmon. Giving him the benefit of the doubt, that is.

"I'll try to resist the temptation," I said.

"Besides that," Harmon said, "I'm really here for business. Right, Suzetta honey? Suzetta is my personal secretary," he told me in a stage aside.

If the woman could type three words a minute, I'd eat the typewriter ribbon. I took a long drink of scotch and said, "Oh, really? That must be fascinating—for both of you. You're here on business?"

Harmon's laugh was much closer to an oink that I had anticipated. "That's right, sweetie—business. You look smart for a woman; tell me what you think about this old house and that prime acreage over that way. You think someone with a little smarts might be able to make a go of it?"

"Eric and Mimi seem to be doing well."

"Kids! They keep worrying about the so-called ambiance

and all that stuff. No, little lady, I'm talking about a right sharp developer who could surround this place with a whole subdivision of houses. Every one of them would have a nice view of the lake and a quarter of an acre of land."

"A subdivision out there?" I echoed, surprised. "It's about fifty feet from the edge of the world. Why would anyone want to live this far from town?"

"It's not that far as your crow flies," Harmon chuckled. He refilled the glasses and slumped back in his chair. Droplets of sweat had popped up on his forehead like blisters, and he pulled out a bandana to wipe them away. A polyester bandana. "As our crow flies, sweetie, it's not far at all," he informed me again.

"I don't see what migration patterns have to do with it," I said. One last glass of scotch and I would leave this porcine chauvinist to fondle whatever part of Suzetta he could alight on in his myopic stupor.

"Your crow won't have to fly," Harmon confided, his voice reduced to a sibilant whisper. "There's going to be a big beautiful highway on the other side of the hill. You'll have your four lanes and your gravel shoulders. It'll take about ten minutes to drive into town on the new highway, and we'll have a quaint little rural community of hundred-thousand-dollar houses on cul-dee-saxes."

"Mimi and Eric are going to sell the Mimosa Inn?"

Suzetta giggled. "They sure are, aren't they, honey bear?"

Harmon took out the bandana and noisily blew his nose. "I told you not to talk about that Suzetta. It's a hush-hush deal."

"Hush-hush," she repeated obediently, nibbling her lip as she tried to print the instructions on her undersized slate. She gave Harmon a puzzled frown. "But you're telling her, Harmon."

"Claire Malloy," I inserted, tired of the conversation and

the insufferable pair. "Thanks for the drink, Harmon, Suzetta. Perhaps I'll see you at dinner."

"Why, you'll see me right here on this here veranda with this here bottle," Harmon chortled, back to his normal bray of a voice. "I'm here to celebrate my deal, and you crazy folks can do all the dee-tecking you want. Harmon Crundall is going to drink scotch with his little girl and watch the sun plop into that pond. But watch out, Miss Claire! I may solve the mystery from my chair, just like that little Belgian guy with the swelled head and the mustache. Make fools of all of you, wouldn't I, Suzetta honey?"

He and Suzetta were laughing as I escaped into the drawing room. I had an urge to take a scalding shower to rid myself of the invisible layer of slime—but that wouldn't solve any murders. It was unfortunate that Harmon was a guest rather than the victim; with foresight, I could solve the murder and drink the evidence.

Before Peter did. I had forgotten about his untimely appearance, but it hadn't been a bad dream. He was standing by the registration desk, deep in discussion with the raven-headed Mimi. I made a dash for the stairs.

"Claire! Have you met our lovely innkeeper?" he called sweetly.

I stopped and smiled, but not at him. "No, not yet. Eric has mentioned you, but we haven't been introduced. I'm Claire Malloy," I said, holding out my hand.

Hers was porcelain, white and smooth, yet surprisingly firm. "I've heard all about you from Eric. In fact, you and your husband comprise most of his fond memories of Farber College. I was so sorry to hear of your husband's accident, but I'm delighted that you could come this weekend."

I looked at Peter as I answered her. "I thought it sounded like a charming idea, so interesting. Although I haven't found any telltale clues yet . . ."

"You will," Mimi said. Her eyes drifted over my shoulder to the doors leading to the porch. "That dreadful man has captured Mrs. Robison-Dewitt. I'd better see if I can do something with him before he sends everyone packing."

"The scotch is likely to solve your problem," I said. "He's already halfway through the bottle; he'll pass out before too long."

Mimi shook her head. "You mustn't underestimate Harmon Crundall. He's a brute and a pig. I wish he'd drink himself to death in the next few hours."

"He's not exactly my Prince Charming, but he's not that bad," I protested. I wondered why I was defending the man.

"You don't know Harmon," Mimi said morosely. She lifted her chin to stare at me, the violet eyes transformed to circles of slate. "Or do you?"

THREE

"**I**'ve never seen that man before in my entire life," I said to Mimi, surprised by her tacit accusation. I was not the only one who was determined to be suspicious; the busboy would probably demand to see my driver's license if I asked for a drink.

Mimi grimaced. "He's a pig. That woman with him is out of a low-budget movie, isn't she? Strictly artificial turf in her yard."

I opened my mouth to agree, then clamped it closed. Mimi had agreed too quickly, had offered the condemnation too easily. Very suspicious. I glanced at Peter to see if he had noticed anything, and met innocent, warm eyes. Just like a painting on velvet—and about as credible.

"Absolutely," I managed to say to Mimi, edging away from them. The game, I reminded myself, was afoot, and the champagne would go to the winner. I stumbled into a barricade behind me. It gasped and began to sputter an incoherent apology.

"Excuse me, I didn't think—I didn't realize that you— oh, dear, I am dreadfully sorry to startle you. I do so—oh!"

The woman gave up and gazed imploringly at me. Her wispy brown hair formed a halo around pale, nondescript features, and her shabby cloth sprouted threads at the seams. There was a faint aroma of mothballs about her, as if she'd been stored for several years in a trunk. I swallowed an urge to tidy her up.

"You will forgive me, won't you?" she pleaded.

Unaccustomed to terrifying undernourished, dowdy women, I nodded. "I ran into you, I'm afraid. I ought to apologize."

The woman shrank back as though I'd bared fangs at her. Her hand was now on her heart, or at least in the general area. Two patches of red appeared on her concave cheeks. "No, I came up behind you, and it was inexcusable of me," she insisted in a ragged whisper as she continued to retreat.

Peter caught her arm before she could stumble over a brass planter. Gently, he said, "Would you like to sit down?"

"No, I couldn't," she gasped. She slipped out of his grip and looked at Mimi, who had been observing the scene with a stunned expression. "You're Mrs. Vanderhan?"

With a tiny jerk, Mimi came out of the trance. "Yes, I am. Are you registered for the weekend?"

"I didn't make a reservation, but I must stay here. It's— it's important, you see, that I stay here. Could I dare presume that you might have an extra room for me?"

"I'm afraid that's impossible."

"I wouldn't mind something small or out of the way," the woman persisted, increasingly agitated. "Perhaps a room over the stable might be available? I could pay whatever you asked, even if it's just for a closet. It's so very important, you see."

Mimi didn't see, nor did I. We both stared at the sad little woman who was begging for a closet as if it were the most crucial thing in the world. Several of the guests had gathered nearby, a row of elderly bunnies intent on a patch of forbidden carrots. I could hear the trickle of salivation.

Peter at last broke the silence, saying, "The inn is sponsoring a special event this weekend, Mrs. . . . ?"

"A convention?" She peered nervously over her shoulder, in case a salesman should pop out of the brass planter to slap a name tag on her lapel or seduce her with spiked punch.

"Not exactly," murmured Mimi. "It's rather complicated, but the fact is that we are filled this weekend. The quarters over the garage are used by the staff, and all of our closets are full of brooms. I'm terribly sorry that we can't accommodate you, Mrs. . . . ?"

I had an urge to try the same ploy, but I was more interested in the address of her mental hospital—from which she clearly had escaped. She had listened to Mimi with growing dread, and now seemed on the verge of a collapse—which would amuse the rubber-neckers behind us, but was apt to disrupt the ambiance.

She breathed for a moment in noisy little gulps, then said, "What about the little bungalows beyond the garden? I will pay whatever you tell me, but it's so dreadfully important."

"We only use them when the inn is filled," Mimi said, "and they're closed now. I suppose we could air one for you, Mrs. . . . ?"

"Smith," the woman quavered. She gave Mimi a pathetically grateful look, nodded at me, and scurried over to the desk to snatch up a battered cloth suitcase. She was through the back door before Mimi could find the registration book.

Mimi gave me a wry smile. "There's not much reason to insist that Mrs. Smith put her name in the book, is there? I'm surprised she didn't try 'Jane Doe.' What a curious creature . . . Why do you think she is so determined to stay here, Claire?"

"Perhaps she's compulsive about croquet," I said, equally mystified but not especially concerned. I had more important things to worry about, so I shifted to an expression of mild curiosity. "Are you in the process of selling the Mimosa Inn to Harmon Crundall?"

Flinching, Mimi moved behind the desk and took several minutes to write Mrs. Smith's name in the registration book. "It's a possibility," she said, her voice so low, I could barely hear her.

"Eric didn't mention it earlier."

"It's not something we enjoy discussing. Last fall, when we wanted to buy the inn, we were a little short on the down payment. Harmon paid us a substantial sum for an option on some land. It's been a slow season, what with the bitterly cold winter and all. We had some severe plumbing problems that played havoc with the budget, and we were unable to buy back the option. Now Harmon has insisted that we allow him to exercise the option on the land that adjoins the inn. Should that happen, the Mimosa Inn would be ruined."

"Dreadful," I murmured encouragingly. I noticed that Peter was eavesdropping and moved closer to the desk. "So that's why he's here this weekend?"

"The option expires Monday at midnight. He brought the contract and papers for us to sign. Our lawyer says we haven't much choice." She looked around the room with a tight frown. "It's not fair. We haven't really had a chance to make a go of the Mimosa Inn. Our bookings are strong for the remainder of the summer and fall, and we ought to show a healthy profit by then."

"But Harmon won't wait?"

"We'll be sitting in the middle of an urban war zone by next spring," Mimi said bitterly. She slammed the book closed. "But you mustn't worry about it, Claire. I'll think of something on my own. Harmon Crundall won't destroy the Mimosa Inn, unless he does it over my dead body—or his!"

Her eyes welled with tears. Covering her mouth with her hand, she dashed into the office. The sound of sobs came through the door, muffled but unmissable. I waited for a moment, then turned toward the stairs.

Peter stepped into my path. "Very interesting," he said with a grin, tilting his head at the closed door.

I sidestepped around him and continued on. "Wasn't it? Of course, she and Eric must be heartbroken about the deal. It's nasty stuff."

"Are you going upstairs to make squiggles in your notebook? I thought we might take a stroll around the grounds. We can search for clues, or simply enjoy the sunshine."

I shot Mr. Amiable a sugary smile. "You go on, Peter. I do have a few things to jot down, but I'll catch up with you in a few minutes. Besides, Caron may be devising some scheme to escape. I need to check on her."

I had no intention of strolling with the man—or searching for clues together. This was a solo flight, and I wasn't going to behave like an ambulatory pigeon. He knew that I knew something; he was hoping to pry it out of me with his broad, warm smiles and sincere gazes. Ha!

On the way upstairs I congratulated myself on the display of self-control. Now that I had recovered from the shock of finding him at the inn, I would try to discover why he was there. But first things first, I told myself as I went into my room.

Caron was gone. The bed was rumpled; the bedspread had been used as a cover and the pillow was on the floor. Her suitcases had been emptied onto all available surfaces, the floor being the most convenient. That much was dictated by her character. Her absence was not, however: I was fairly certain she hadn't come downstairs for the lecture nor slipped away for a swim in the lake. Food was out, due to the diet.

· I picked up the pillow and tossed it on the bed, exposing a folded sheet of paper on the floor. Glumly anticipating a suicide note from Caron, I opened it and read: "Vital clue: Tues. a hobo collapsed nearby."

Very curious—and very suspicious. It made no sense whatsoever, but its intent was clear. I had allowed myself to be distracted by Peter's appearance and the crazy scenes downstairs. This was the first clue; all I had to do was decipher it before any of my fellow sleuths . . . or Peter. Champagne would surely follow. I read it several times.

"Vital clue: Tues. a hobo collapsed nearby."

I went to the window and looked down at the serene scene below. The grassy beach was again populated by a series of lumpy figures, a miniaturized mountain range of broiled flesh. None of them resembled a hobo, rehabilitated or not. How was I to determine what had happened three days ago?

Eric was in the middle of the croquet court with one of the elderly couples. They practiced strokes, then took positions around the court. A blue ball rolled through a wicket. A yellow ball attempted to follow, but bounced back and rolled to a stop against the rail. A surprisingly colorful expletive drifted up to my window.

Farther down the lawn, Peter was in conversation with Mrs. Robison-Dewitt, which I found more than a bit irritating. It hadn't taken him long to form a new alliance, I thought in a petty voice. The two of them deserved each other: She could be Watson to his Holmes, if she didn't prim him to death in the process.

But where was Caron?

I peered under the bed in case she was attempting some nonsense, say only clean floor, and stood up. Harmon's name went into my notebook, along with Suzetta's. Mrs. Smith was noted with a question mark. The clue was refolded and tucked in my pocket. Feeling competent if not befuddled, I left the bedroom.

As I reached the top of the stairs, I saw a figure crawling down the corridor on its hands and knees. Very suspicious. Entranced, I tiptoed behind the figure, which appeared to be a middle-aged man with a dauntingly broad posterior.

Which wiggled as we progressed down the hall. If he had possessed a tail, it would have waggled.

When he reached the wall, he turned and bumped into my shins. He looked up in alarm. I gave him a polite smile and said, "Hello. Did you find any blood-stained dustballs?"

He scrambled to his feet and edged around me, his eyes cold and accusing. "I thought I might have dropped something," he muttered as he pushed past me. He ducked into one of the bedrooms and slammed the door.

I was not fooled by the lame explanation, but I doubted that I would find anything of interest along the floorboard. Leaving the crawler to his dirty-kneed modus operandi, I continued downstairs to find Caron. Or a clue. The latter was more important.

The drawing room was unpopulated, but I heard voices in the dining room. There, to my delight, I found that a portable bar had been rolled in. Several of the guests clutched cocktails. A bartender had been put to work and was fending off the good-natured rush with laughter—and liquor.

"Hi," he said as I approached with a hungry look. "You don't look like a sherry sort of person. What can I get for you?"

He was well under thirty. His tanned face and sun-bleached blond hair gave him the appearance of a California beach boy, which was somewhat improbable a thousand miles inland. He did have the muscles and white teeth; all he lacked was a surfboard. Did I care?

"A small scotch and water," I said. "What happened to the sherry-only dictum?"

"Mimi sensed a potential rebellion in the ranks and decided to open the bar. Shall I put this on your tab?" he said, pushing a glass across the bar.

I decided that Mimi was probably hoping to make a fortune before Monday in order to thwart the Crundall scheme. On the other hand, it was an admirable idea. "I didn't see you earlier," I said idly.

"I went into town after lunch. I do most of the shopping and run errands as needed. How's the murder going?"

"We're all still breathing. I did find a clue in my room, but I can't figure it out—yet. Do you serve hints?"

His white teeth contrasted with his tan. Winking at me, he scooped up a few olives from a dish and began to juggle them with amazing competence. "Olives, onions, or oranges," he said, "but no hints. I'm under orders—and I don't really know anything, anyway. I'm only hired help."

Mesmerized by the flying olives, I nodded dumbly and then forced myself to leave the dining room. Strange guests, juggling bartenders, insidious business schemes, incomprehensible clues on the bedroom floor. A murder was definitely in the making. I loved it.

Harmon and Suzetta were still on the porch. The bottle was more than half full, which meant it had been exchanged with a depleted one. Suzetta was concentrating on her toenails. Harmon gave me a blurry grin, but I hurried down the steps before he could offer an equally blurry invitation to join them.

Peter and Eric stood in the middle of the croquet court, while Caron watched from a shady seat against the lattice wall that surrounded the underside of the porch. She resembled a teenaged, freckled Buddha. I gave her a vague wave and tried to veer around the court before I was snagged.

"Claire!" Eric called. "Come play croquet with us."

"Later," I answered over my shoulder. I would go to the garden, I decided, and reread the clue until it made sense. If necessary, I would search the woods for pieces of a hobo. Then—

"One little game, Claire," Eric pleaded. "We need another person to have a foursome. This gentleman is a beginner, so you needn't be intimidated."

Gentleman, my fanny. I went back to the court and yanked a mallet from the cart. "One quick game, Eric." I flashed a pseudo-grin at Peter Rosen. "I won't be intimidated. The gentleman talks a good game, but he's liable to knock his balls in the lake. Now, what do I do?"

Eric came over and showed me how to hold the mallet. I put one ball neatly through a wicket, straightened up and said, "Well, are we ready to play?"

Peter took careful aim and sent his ball into mine. They clinked woodenly. "I'm ready, Eric. What happened to our fourth?"

"Here she comes," Eric replied absently, gathering up the balls to set them near a brightly striped wooden post.

Mrs. Robison-Dewitt came down the steps, spotted me, and drew herself to a halt. We stared at each other. Her mouth tightened until it disappeared into a web of wrinkles, and her nostrils quivered with displeasure. The gesture was familiar, and not popular.

"*She* is going to play?" Mrs. Robison-Dewitt snorted.

Eric looked bewildered; Peter looked quietly convulsed with laughter, although he managed to restrain himself from audible disgrace. I suspect I looked as pleased as the dear old battleship, but I managed a cool expression.

"I was collared into it," I said, "but I'll be glad to withdraw, if you're concerned about your personal safety. One never quite knows where one's shots will go."

Eric grabbed a mallet and sent his ball through the first two wickets. "Your turn," he told Peter brightly.

Mrs. Robison-Dewitt turned out to be a mean croquet player. My ball was knocked about the court at every opportunity, and once rolled within inches of the lake. We played in silence, each intent on damaging each other's positions as maliciously as possible. I was not a natural, but I managed to do adequately. On the sidelines, Caron observed our progress with a glum expression.

After an hour, Eric finally won. Mrs. Robison-Dewitt nodded at him, replaced her mallet, and stalked into the inn. Peter was discussing strategy with Eric as I went over to talk to Caron.

"Haven't you found anything to do yet?" I asked her.

"No, I haven't. The people running this farce aren't going to have to murder anyone; I'm going to expire from boredom any second now. The youngest guest is about seventy years old, Mother. I feel as though I'm at a retirement home."

I was thirty-nine years old. That gave me over thirty years to meet Caron's criterion for the retirement home, but I decided to overlook it. Dropping to the grass beside her, I pulled the clue out of my pocket. "In the midst of the tragic ennui, see if you can figure this out," I suggested.

In spite of herself, Caron glanced at it. "Was there a hobo in the area? Wait a minute—that sounds like a cryptic clue."

"I found it cryptic, to say the least."

"No, Mother, I mean a cryptic crossword clue." She took the paper to study it more closely. "The word 'collapsed' is the tip-off that the beginning of the sentence is an anagram. We have to rearrange the letters in the 'Tues. a hobo' to get . . . boathouse!"

I grabbed the paper back. "You're right, Caron. There must be something in the boathouse. Do you want to go poke around with me? You're much better at crossword clues than I."

Caron stretched and stood up. "I think I'll take a nap. See you later, Miss Marple." She went up the steps and disappeared into the house.

The boathouse, I told myself as I hurriedly scrambled to my feet. I glanced at Peter, who was still talking to Eric. I did not want any uninvited guests tagging along, although I would have welcomed Caron's cryptic expertise. The child does amaze at times.

I had reached the far side of the court when a bellow stopped me. The bellower was Harmon Crundall—and the bellowee the mysterious Mrs. Smith. She stood in the middle of the porch, the pitiful suitcase in one hand and an equally pitiful purse in the other. Her face was as white as the gingerbread trim, but it was rapidly changing to match the gray of the siding. Harmon, on the other hand, had opted for a patchy cerise.

"Bella! How dare you come here, you mousy pile of rags! If I had wanted to see you—and I don't—I would have brought you here!" he roared. If she had been a house made of straw, she would have been blown over the rail.

"I had to come, Harmon."

"You—had—to—come? You didn't have to come, Bella! I told you to stay home and do some housework; I want you to get out of here this minute and wait at the house! I'll see you Monday—if you're lucky!" Harmon slammed the bottle down to emphasize his rage. Golden liquid gurgled over the top and drenched his hand.

"Oh my God," Eric said in an underbreath. He started for the porch, although I couldn't see what he could do. Mimi came out of the drawing room door with Nickie Merrick on her heels.

"Leave!" Harmon roared. He pointed at the lake as if expecting the waters to part and produce your four-lane highway with your gravel shoulders.

Although the recipient of his rage was trembling, her jaw crept out to a mulish position, and she seemed to take on a few inches of stature. "I will not leave, Harmon. I have as much right to be here as you. More, since I didn't bring a floozy with me!"

Suzetta jerked herself up. "Harmon, are you going to let her talk to me like that? I think it's disgraceful that your wife would follow you on a business trip, and I also think it's disgraceful that you let her call me nasty names."

A lot of cerebration for the blonde, I told myself as I moved closer to the porch. It was infinitely more intriguing than croquet—and very suspicious. Our Mrs. Smith was obviously Mrs. Bella Crundall. An unfortunate state of affairs.

Harmon had difficulty dealing with the situation, having

spent several hours pickling his brain. "Suzetta baby, give me a minute to think of something. I'm sure Bela didn't mean to call you a floozy, honey bunch. She knows that you're my secretary." He tried to focus his eyes on Bella without much success. "This is business, Bela. Suzetta has to type some papers for me."

"Oh, Harmon," Bella groaned. She ran down the steps to the path that would ultimately take her to the bungalows. We all stared at her flapping coat until she was gone. All of us except Suzetta, who I noticed was busy repairing her lipstick with an unconcerned air.

Mimi stepped forward. "Mr. Crundall, we cannot allow this kind of scene at the Mimosa Inn. Our guests are disturbed, and frankly so am I. Perhaps it would be better if you and Miss Price were to leave."

"I'm not leaving anywhere," Harmon rumbled in a thunderous voice. "I'm going to be here Monday morning to finish our deal. If you don't like it, Mrs. Vanderhan honey, you can go suck a mimosa leaf!"

He stumbled to his feet and staggered toward the drawing room door. "Come on, Suzetta, we're going to sit in the bar. I'm tired of waiting for ice; maybe that bartender can juggle it into my glass faster if we sit inside."

Suzetta followed at a leisurely pace, preening in the attention of the spectators. When the door closed, I heard the sound of twenty-odd breaths being released. Quite a drama, I concluded thoughtfully. The imprudent husband, the wife, the bubble-headed blonde. A trite but nevertheless intriguing triangle.

Peter came over to me. "Intrigued?"

"Not in the least," I said with a cool, if mendacious, smile. "It's simply a pathetic little situation that should not have been aired in public. The poor woman was ill-advised to follow her husband, and he was ill-advised to raise such hell about it. Suzetta was ill-advised at birth. But it is none of our business and, if you'll excuse me, I'm going for a walk."

Smiling to myself, I drifted away from him. Smiling to himself, he caught up with me. Damn. We walked in silence for several minutes, arriving at last at the marble cherub in the garden. I had forced myself not to look at the boathouse when we passed it, but I was eager to examine it—alone. I wasn't eager to share Caron's brilliant deductions with anyone, especially Supercop.

"I believe that's Cupid, the Roman love imp," he said, pointing at the statue. "Do you think it's an omen?"

"No, I think it's a mildly vulgar statue of a little boy who should have put on clothes before climbing on a pedestal. Why don't you take a hike—with Mrs. Robison-Dewitt?"

"One of your admirers?"

"Not precisely, but clearly one of yours. You shouldn't let such a golden opportunity to be worshiped slip away. She may not have Suzetta's curves, but I'm sure she has admirable qualities. If nothing else, she might feature you in the *Ozark Chronicle*. You should be the cover boy for the autumn edition. I'd even buy a copy, just to keep under my pillow."

"Claire, I wish you'd relax," he said. He caught my hand and led me to a stone bench. I permitted the presumptuous familarity out of curiosity. Or so I told myself.

"Then explain why you came," I demanded, perching on one end of the bench, the better to escape should the necessity arise.

"I can't, Claire. It has to do with a long-term investigation, but I'm not at liberty to discuss it. There are some unsavory people involved; it might be dangerous for you to have any information about the case."

"Here? At the Mimosa Inn? I don't believe you, Peter. I think you came simply to . . ."

"To show you up?"

"Which is futile. I am going to solve the murder and win

the champagne. I may also decide to go after the croquet championship."

"Oh, really?" Eyebrows rose like fermatas.

I knew he was baiting me, but I couldn't stop myself. "Yes, really, Peter Rosen. Would you like to make a side bet about the murder solution?"

"That would certainly spice up the drama, wouldn't it? What do you suggest we bet?"

"Whatever you can afford to lose," I suggested sweetly.

"All I possess is my virtue—but I'm willing to risk it."

"I didn't realize you had any vestiges of virtue. A dinner might be more appropriate, or straightforward currency," I said. Or dithered.

"Dinner it is," Peter said. "The loser will prepare an extravagant meal for the winner, seven courses with wine for each. We'll leave the question of virtue for a later discussion."

"Fine. Now why don't you run along and pretend you're on the trail of a real criminal. I'd like to sit here by myself. I need to ponder my plan of action." And get to the boathouse . . . alone.

His expression abruptly sober, he stood up and said, "There is no pretense, Claire. But I want you to promise me to focus all your energy on solving the mock murder, and forget what I said about the investigation. Okay?"

I drew a big X on my chest as I crossed my fingers behind my back. "Absolutely."

FOUR

After Peter left, I went back to the boathouse. It was a small white building, freshly whitewashed but still in need of general repairs—as we all are at times. I slipped inside and closed the door. Light fell through cracks in the walls, casting yellow stripes on squatty cardboard boxes, piles of paddles, and musty tarps. Water lapped quietly in two slips, one empty and the other protecting a dilapidated rowboat with a puddle of foul water in its bottom.

My nose began to tingle with an incipient sneeze. I warned it to behave as I investigated the piles of clutter, praying there would be no fuzzy little things with four (or more) legs to be encountered. Nothing. As I turned to leave, the sneeze came. I stopped to wipe my eyes and saw on the back of the door a few words scrawled with a pencil.

"Aha!" I said in quiet triumph. The next clue was uncovered. It took me a few minutes to read the words in the dim light, but at last I made them out and faithfully recorded them in my notebook: "The rickety building holds the answer."

Wonderful. I was in the only rickety building in sight,

and I was fairly sure I hadn't overlooked anything of importance. The word "rickety" could be arranged to read "tickery" or "cry kite," but that seemed farfetched. I gave up on anagrams. One could, I supposed, be smothered with a canvas tarp or bludgeoned with a canoe paddle. No one had, as far as I knew.

I forced myself to my hands and knees. Trying not to notice the pain to said parts of my anatomy, I crawled over every last inch of floor and squeamishly poked a finger in every last inky corner. I found countless cobwebs, a toothless comb, a beerless beer can, and a limitless amount of dust. The last was my downfall.

I was kneeling on the floor, sneezing hysterically, when the door opened. The rectangle of sunlight caught me in the undignified pose, but it was not enough to interrupt the sneezes. My eyes were blinded with tears; my nose produced a spasm of outrage about every three seconds. It was a charming picture, I concluded as I helplessly waited out the staccato barrage.

At last things quieted down. I wiped my eyes and stood up. A bewildered Nickie Merrick was frozen in the doorway.

"Claire, are you okay?"

I hesitated in order to confirm that the fireworks were totally over, then said, "Hello, Nickie. It seems that I'm allergic to whatever is growing in dark corners. There aren't any clues in here, but there is something worth further study in terms of chemical warfare. That much I have deduced. It's safe to come in now." I punctuated the promise with a sneeze.

"No, don't let me interrupt you; I was just wandering about to see how the sleuths were doing. Have you made any progress with the clues?"

"Some, but I'm ready to leave," I admitted. We walked to the house together. When we reached the porch, I said, "Are you playing Scotland Yard at the high tea? George

Gideon, or a milder sort such as Roderick Allyn or Henry Tibbet?"

"Only if I can find my knickers and my plimsolls. For whom shall I scan the crowd? A sleek Cordelia Grey or a determined Harriet Vane?"

"An uninspired but sincere Miss Marple. If you'll excuse me, it's time to don the orthopedic shoes with the crepe soles and fetch my knitting—after a quick shower."

All of which I did. Afterwards, I sat in front of the dressing table and went so far as to powder my hair into a temporary gray. Caron napped through the preparations. Although I was tempted to awaken her in order to discuss the ominous words on the boathouse door (a nice ring), I let her sleep. I did, however, put my notebook on the dressing table in case she rallied while I was downstairs. "The rickety building holds the answer." Unless and somehow smug, I told myself glumly as I left the room for the ritual of high tea. A charming excuse for a fourth meal; no wonder our English cousins have well-rounded, rosy cheeks.

I met several of my cohorts in the hallway, specifically two caped Sherlock Holmeses, an unshaven man in a trenchcoat who had glued a cigarette to his lower lip—and a gaggle of gray-headed women with knitting bags. We trooped out to the porch. More gray-headed women with knitting bags were tearing into cucumber sandwiches and scones. Pinkies were curled like stout commas.

We were not amused. Feeling like an instant replay, I took a cup and saucer from Mimi, who was presiding over a silver tea service, loaded up a plate with goodies, and eased through the crowd to the end of the porch and a broad, inviting swing.

An Oriental gentleman in a white coat and string bow tie twinkled at me over a sliver of walnut cake. "Miss Marple?"

"Good guess," I sighed. "Are you Charlie Chan?"

The cup clattered on his saucer. "I am Hercule Poirot," he snorted. In farewell.

As a wave of heat rushed up my neck, a black man came out of the crowd and joined me. He ran his eyes over my longish black dress, lace collar, and cardigan sweater. "Miss Marple?" he hazarded.

"Good guess. Hercule Poirot?"

His cup clattered, too. "Sam Spade," he corrected me haughtily as he retreated.

I was doing wonderfully. Zero out of two, and hostility to boot. Clearly, I should cease the game and spend my idle moments thinking about the rickety-building clue. As much as I adored tea, I could more profitably pass the time sneezing in the boathouse—or rattling Caron into a more helpful frame of mind.

Before I could finish my tea and escape, Peter wormed his way through the crowd. He smiled at my costume, but made no comment. He wore the same clothes he had been in earlier, a knit shirt and chino pants. Designer sneakers, of course.

"Who are you supposed to be?" I asked politely.

"Peter Wimsey."

"Lord Peter Wimsey does not skulk about in shirts with alligators on the front. His valet would never permit it."

"I'm undercover," he explained with facetious sincerity.

I was trying to decide whether or not he deserved a laugh, when Nickie Merrick came through the crowd. "Did I hear you say that you were undercover, Lieutenant Rosen?" he said, an unpleasant smile on his face.

"That's right, Merrick."

The two men studied each other, as if they were mongrels in front of a succulent bone. For a brief moment, I flattered myself that I was the bone under contention, but let the image evaporate as the seconds stretched into decidedly uneasy minutes. Murder seemed in the making, and it would occur before my eyes if I didn't do something to ease the tension.

"He's Peter Wimsey," I tried with a gay laugh.

"Is he?" said Nickie. No gay laugh followed.

"His valet was held up at the deer crossing," I continued in the same bright voice. Clever, clever Claire. "When the poor man arrives, he'll be scandalized, won't he, Lord Peter?"

Peter gave Nickie one final glance, then smiled at me. "I like the 'Lord Peter' title, Claire. I may have it put on my credit cards when I get back home."

"To Farberville, Lieutenant?" said Nickie.

Peter nodded. Nickie spun on his heel and pushed his way through the wall of bodies to the door. It slammed behind him, causing several unwary Marples to jiggle their teacups in alarm.

"What was that about?" I asked.

"Scotland Yard doesn't seem to appreciate the competition from the Farberville CID. He doesn't realize that with you here, my chances of solving anything are noticeably diminished."

"Oh?" I said. I was about to add a further comment when Mrs. Robison-Dewitt appeared. She was wearing a longish black dress with a lace collar, a cardigan sweater, and orthopedic shoes with crepe soles. She held a knitting bag in one hand. She hadn't powdered her hair, but she hadn't needed any theatrical assistance there.

Two mirror images, right down to the strained attempts to produce socially acceptable nods. The Bobbsey twins in drag. Tweedledee and Tweedledum, just as the black bird filled the sky.

She took in my costume in a single look that felt like a toothpick in my carotid artery. "How interesting you look, Mrs. Malloy," she whinnied through her nose. "Whom did you intend to represent?"

"Nero Wolfe," I told her levelly. "This is Archie Goodwin, but I believe you two have already met."

"Mr. Goodwin, so pleased to see you again." She wasn't.

The porch was glazing over with ice. Peter grabbed me and tugged me through the crowd. Muffled noises came from his throat, but he managed to hold in the laughter until we reached the drawing room.

"Nero Wolfe?" he sputtered.

I disengaged my arm and sat on a brocade settee. "That woman ought to be put out to pasture. She's been snorting at me since I arrived. How dare she show up in my costume."

"She's undoubtedly echoing that sentiment to whoever will listen. After the lecture, she asked me with great seriousness if you might have the symptoms of a sociopath. A homicidal sociopath, if I recall. I told her that your psychiatrist was fairly certain that you were unlikely to attack anyone except for family members and close friends. I don't think she found comfort in the diagnosis."

It was my turn to sputter, and I did. "You said what?"

"I had to say something."

"You did not have to say all that nonsense about psychiatrists or imply that I am prone to murder my relatives," I said. "If the inclination should occur, it will center on detectives who go around slandering innocent people!"

"Innocent?"

"This is a drawing room, not an echo chamber. I am going upstairs to change clothes and study all the clues I've thus far deciphered. You might utilize the time with a cookbook, since you're going to need some recipes in the immediate future!"

I stomped up the stairs, my shoulders squared and my head erect. Dangerous in that I couldn't see my feet over my nose, but well worth the minor peril. I bumped into Harmon and Suzetta halfway up the stairs. Harmon had his pudgy fingers clamped tightly around the bannister, which was wise. He appeared to be on another planet, where he was apt to encounter little green men along with the notorious pink elephants.

Suzetta was wearing a black bikini, with black and white scarves artistically draped over her basically bare body. Eye makeup had been applied with a leaden hand. A paste emerald glittered from her navel.

"I just adore costume parties!" she confided with a giggle. "Do you recognize me? I'm a harem girl—or a Harmon girl! Isn't that the cutest joke?"

"The cutest," I agreed gravely. "Do find Mrs. Robison-Dewitt and see if she can guess what you are; she'll be so gratified, and she just adores puns."

Suzetta produced a blank look. Long past the blank stage, Harmon grabbed her waist. "Lez go, honey bunch. Honey bear wants a little drink."

Waving her eyelashes in farewell, Suzetta obediently tripped down the stairs. If there were a troll under the staircase, he would have been thrilled with the tender flesh, ninety-five percent of it conveniently exposed. Honey bear was already marinated.

My thoughts returned to Peter Rosen's jibe. "Innocent?" he had drawled in mocking disbelief. And telling the battleship that my psychiatrist was almost sure I wouldn't attack a stranger! She was now undoubtedly convinced I was Farberville's version of Lizzie Borden. Peter deserved all eighty of the whacks.

I stormed into the room and slammed the door. Caron lay in bed, a book balanced on her knee.

"Did you look at this?" I demanded belligerently as I snatched up my notebook to flap it at her. "Are you going to help me with the murder or not?"

Caron's lip floated downward as she took in my costume and prematurely gray hair. If it was gray because of the powder. After the episode on the porch, I wouldn't have been too surprised if the gray failed to brush out. Ever.

"Mother?" she whispered.

"No, Jane Fonda! Listen, Caron, I wish you'd pull yourself out of this self-imposed lethargy and help me with the clues. You're liable to ruin the mattress if you stay there indefinitely. Furthermore, I—"

"What on earth is wrong with you?" Caron interrupted calmly. "You sound like a harpy."

She had a point. I made a face in apology and sat down to brush the powder out of my hair. Despite my fears, my reddish hair soon reappeared as my shoulders disappeared under a talcum snowfall. It helped to calm me down, and when I finally turned around, my voice was back to normal.

"Sorry, dear. High tea has never been my style." I told her about the encounters with Hercule and Sam Spade, which resulted in a round of uncontrollable giggles from her and a few from me. Mrs. Robison-Dewitt was good for a second round. Then Caron returned to her book, and I opted for a soothing bath with my notebook propped on a soapy knee. Afterwards, I put on a wool dress and we went downstairs for dinner.

Some of the guests had changed clothes, but many of them were still in costume. Nickie sat at the head of a table of Marples as though he were the captian of a cruise ship. In one corner, the blond bartender tossed olives in the air between orders; Eric was busy uncorking bottles of wine. Mimi caught Caron and me at the dining-room door and led us toward a table for eight.

"Found any clues?" she asked as we moved between the tables.

I made a noncommittal reply. Caron and I found ourselves sitting with a depressed Marple, a food-splattered Dover, the Oriental Hercule—and the Peter Wimsey-Rosen. While Caron tired not to giggle, I avoided everyone by escaping into the menu. After orders had been given, we began a desultory conversation about the scheduled croquet tournament.

"Oh, Harmon," trilled a voice from the doorway, "isn't this just terribly nice! Wherever shall we sit?"

A shudder went around the table, since there were two

empty chairs. Inevitably, Suzetta spotted them and dragged an anesthetized Harmon Crundall across the dining room. She wore a scarlet dress, slightly more conventional than the harem outfit. The neckline was more of a waistline, however, and the flesh count still hovered above the seventy-percent mark.

Peter sucked in a breath as she leaned over him and said, "Do you mind if we sit here?"

"By all means," he managed to say, once his eyeballs returned to their proper location.

Harmon thudded into one of the chairs. He tried to pat the seat next to him, but his hand swished past the edge and he almost toppled over. With a faint squeak, Suzetta sat down.

When the waiter came, she ordered for both of them, although it was obvious that Harmon was far beyond the food-as-redemption stage. His face was blotched, his lips flecked with spittle. It was only a matter of time before the fall from grace.

Those of us at the table again took up the topic of croquet rules, politely ignoring the occasional belch from Harmon and the increasingly acerbic whispers from his companion. Caron was mortified by the adult antics; I could sense her bristle with indignation. When dinner arrived, we began to eat with ravenous concentration, as if we hadn't been stuffing ourselves with tea-party food earlier.

Harmon looked at his plate. "Waz that?"

"Dinner, Harmon. Please try to eat something, honey bear," Suzetta said, nudging him upright and tucking a napkin in his collar. A bib did seem appropriate.

"Can't eat thiz. Might be drugged, ya know. Lez ask that man—he's a cop and he oughta know about that stuff. Isn't that right, Mr. Policeman?"

"I believe it's safe," Peter said, puzzled.

"Eat, Harmon," Suzetta commanded in a low voice. "It may help you feel a teensy bit better."

Harmon managed to find his fork, but its purpose eluded him. He was tapping it on the edge of the table and

humming an accompaniment when Mrs. Bella Crundall
came into the room, spotted him, and crossed to his chair.

"Oh, Harmon, how could you?"

"Waz that?" Harmon blinked at the shadow across his
plate. "Iz that some kinda eclipse?"

"You're drunk," said Bella Crundall, her expression
surprisingly harsh. She rapped her hasband's sagging
shoulder. "You ought to lie down, Harmon—and you ought
to be ashamed of yourself! I have already accepted the fact
that our marriage is over, ruined by your self-centered,
piggish desire to recapture your youth by taking up with
some girl young enough to be your daughter."

"Suzetta my sec'ertary," he protested petulantly.

"You're hopeless, and the only thing I can do to avoid
being pulled into your whirlpool of degradation is to divorce
you."

He gave her a crafty, albeit lopsided, smile. "You better
not divorce me, Bella. I'm going to divorce you first, and
then I'm going tell my policeman—I mean my lawyer—
whoever . . . Anyway, I'm going to put ever'thing in
Suzetta's name. You won't get a penny of my money. You'll
be a pooper!"

"I doubt I'll be a pauper, Harmon Crundall. You, on the
other hand, are apt to end up in a hospital with a terminal
liver ailment. I hope this girl will be at your bedside when
your time comes. I shall not!" Bella shot Suzetta a pitying
look and swooped out of the dining room, a schooner under
full sail.

I wanted to applaud, but it seemed inappropriate. I went
back to my broiled trout, carefully keeping my face
lowered. Gradually, the murmur of conversation started up
once more. Harmon was befuddled but quiet, and Suzetta,
her cheeks pink, began to eat.

As soon as I was finished, I nudged Caron and we stood
up. We took a few steps toward the doorway, but were

stopped by a peculiar, slushy sound from behind us. Mystified, I looked over my shoulder.

Harmon Crundall had taken a swan dive into his plate. His nose was embedded in the potatoes au gratin; a tidbit of lettuce dangled from one ear. The rhythmic drone of a chainsaw filled the air as he began to snore.

Suzetta looked at him, then methodically ate the final bite on her plate and folded her napkin. "Poor Harmon's exhausted from all his work. He just works so hard, and then needs a tiny nap," she explained in a serene voice, as if he weren't in immediate danger of suffocating on a lungful of cheese sauce.

Mimi hurried over, and the two women managed to extricate Harmon from his dinner. Suzetta flicked the lettuce leaf off his ear, dabbed his chin with a napkin, and took his arm. Grimacing under the inert load, they steered him out of the dining room and up the stairs. The rest of us gaped like craniate vertebrates. Caron was visibly appalled; I could hardly wait to hear her condemnation of the episode and of adults as a species.

Nickie Merrick tapped his fork on a glass and said, "Please don't worry about Mr. Crundall; he's on his way to bed, I'm sure. The movie will start promptly at ten o'clock. The busboys will have to move the chairs into the drawing room, so please wait on the porch. Bruce will be serving cordials to those who wish an after-dinner drink."

We all went to the porch, where our juggling bartender poured generous belts of brandy. My dinner companions formed a circle on one end of the porch and all agreed that Harmon's behavior was disgraceful. The absent Bella received a great deal of tongue-clucking and sympathy. When the subject had been thoroughly analyzed, I asked if anyone had solved any cryptic clues. The group disbanded as if I'd mentioned herpes.

Only Peter remained. "So who do you think is to be the ill-fated victim?"

"Harmon, possibly," I said. "If anyone deserves to be murdered, it's that horrible man. But I'm not sure whether he's who he says he is, or is an actor in the mock murder. I'm nurturing a wild hope that Mrs. Robison-Dewitt will be discovered in the classic death pose. She purports to be from some magazine, but I've never heard of it. Do you think she's legitimate?" I mentally gave myself a pat on the back for the timely red herring.

"Can't tell the players without a scorecard," Peter said. He started to add something, but looked over my shoulder and closed his mouth.

I followed his eyes. Suzetta and Mimi stood in the middle of the staircase, deep in conversation. Suzetta looked almost human; her eyelashes were at rest and her kittenish expression had been replaced with a pensive frown. Mimi shook her head in response to something Suzetta said. Suzetta put her hands on the other woman's shoulders and repeated something with noticeably urgency. Again, Mimi shook her head, then pulled away and ran back upstairs.

Suzetta stared after her, now indecisive and quite worried. Then, as if cued by a whisper from off stage, she resumed the brainless pose and pranced down the stairs. "Is it show time?" she asked, loudly enough to be heard on the porch, or across the lake if the bullfrogs were listening.

Before she reached the door, Nickie Merrick strode into the middle of the room and grabbed her arm. He muttered something in her ear that unsettled her, then shoved her toward the door that led to the porch. I caught a glimpse of her white face before she moved out of view. Seconds later, I heard her announce that the movie would begin in only a teeny little second and that she just adored movies, didn't everyone?

I carefully avoided looking at Peter as we went into the drawing room. Caron informed me that she was not about to watch some horrid old movie and went upstairs to call Inez, or so I suspected. Praying the telephone bill would not rival that for the room, I allowed Peter to find chairs for us. Nickie made a few introductory comments about Agatha Christie while Eric took charge of the projector. The lights went out; the movie began.

I tried to keep my eyes open as the fabled Orient Express roared down the tracks, but I dozed off before Hercule could twirl his mustache over a bona fide corpse. From time to time I was aware of shuffled movement in the rows behind us, and I dreamily imagined parallel scenes of mayhen. taking place in the dark room.

I was in the middle of an improbable scenario in the boathouse, complete with oversized spiders using all eight legs to strangle a red-nosed Harmon, while Bella rapped him on the shoulder with a pooper-scooper and demanded a divorce, when Peter shook my shoulder.

"Is he dead yet?" I grumbled.

"Not that I know of. In any case, the movie is over and you're ready for bed."

"This time you may be right—but don't let it go to your head."

Peter pulled me to my feet and kept one arm around my waist until we reached the safety of the second-floor landing. At my door, he gave me a quick kiss on the cheek and pushed me inside. I muzzily noted that Caron was asleep in the middle of the bed. The telephone was on the floor nearby—a bad sign for my checkbook.

I undressed and collapsed beside her. Caron protested but at last ceded two or three inches. I pulled the pillow under my head, punched it into shape, tugged the blanket under my chin, and blissfully closed my eyes.

"Night," I murmured through a yawn.

Thirty minutes later I was still wide awake. I turned on the bedside lamp and read for a while. That managed to rouse me to a state of total alertness. I turned off the light and lay back to listen to the cacophony of crickets, owls, whippoorwills, tree frogs, and other equally dissonant serenaders. After I had tried every sleep-inducing technique I knew short of suicide, I got out of bed and put on a robe.

It was, I discovered, almost one o'clock. I decided the fresh air was responsible for my restlessness and resolved not to breathe any more of it than necessary. In the meantime, I had several hours of free time on my hands—and no late movie to watch.

My stomach made a frivolous suggestion. Unable to think of anything more diverting, I decided to go to the kitchen and see if there might be a neglected plate of scones on the counter. I closed the door behind me and crept down the hall in my bare feet, guided by a dim light from each end of the corridor. Snores and snuffles now joined the outside music. The bucolic countryside, I realized wryly, was more populous than I had ever suspected—and a good deal less peaceful.

A mischievous urge to scream came to mind. Bedroom doors would fly open; sluggish faces would peer into the corridor in hopes of a blood-drenched corpse and a hovering suspect. I would make a pretense of having just dashed out of my room, and would offer a garbled story about a man in a black cloak. Then—

A door closed in the darkness below.

My foot jerked off the first step as though it had touched a burner on a stove. I peered over the bannister at unmoving, misshapen humps of furniture. Squinting did not help. I wiggled my toes. My foot had decided not to cooperate and was firmly entrenched in the sanctuary of midair. If I held the teetery pose much longer, I was apt to fall down the stairs, but I couldn't bring myself to move.

In the middle of all this internal debate, a blond head moved across the area at the bottom of the staircase. The small lamp on the desk caught the swish of Suzetta's scarlet skirt before she vanished from view. The door that led to the parking area opened and closed with diminutive clicks.

Relieved, my foot agreed to meet the carpet. I crept down

the stairs to follow the blonde, all the while smugly picturing Peter's expression when I announced that I had solved the mock murder in the middle of the night. I had suspected that Suzetta did not ring true, and now I had proof. Dopey blondes do not prowl under the cover of night.

I went to a back window and looked out at the depressingly deserted parking area beside the stable. As I stared at the scene, I heard a low rumble that echoed like a distant thunderstorm, although no flicker of lightning had preceded it. I continued to watch, hoping for a flash of scarlet, but Suzetta had vanished—permanently, it seemed. Her destination was as puzzling as the cryptic clues. No light shone from the upper story of the stable, nor did anyone slither from shadow to shadow. No one did anything that I could see.

After ten futile minutes, I reluctantly gave up and started for the kitchen. If I couldn't solve a crime, I could at least console myself with a scone and a glass of milk.

From the darkness, a figure stepped into my path. My nose bounced off a pajama-clad chest.

"Claire?" Peter hissed incredulously.

I gingerly explored the bridge of my nose. "Well, it's not Ellery Queen. Didn't your mother ever teach you not to creep around in your bare feet and frighten people?"

"What do you think you're doing?" More hiss.

"Oh, go to bed!" I hissed in reply. I stomped upstairs and did exactly as I suggested to him.

FIVE

The next morning the main event at last occurred. Eric came into the dining room with a pale, worried face and said, "I'm sorry to disrupt your breakfast, but a terrible thing has happened. At about seven o'clock this morning, the gardener found Harmon Crundall on the floor of the boathouse. Mr. Crundall—he was—I'm afraid—well, he's dead."

A happy little shiver rounded the room. I slipped out my notebook and held it in my lap. I presumed I was slightly ahead of the others in sorting out the suspects, due to both my keen powers of observation and my fortuitous midnight prowl the previous night, even though it had led to no startling insights. I could almost taste the champagne. Perhaps I wouldn't make poor Peter do the cooking. After all, a woman's place may be in the kitchen—as long as she's fixing crow á la king, with humble pie for dessert. He'd get to eat every bite of it, while I basked in the glow of the candlelight. I am such an incurable romantic.

Eric gave us a moment to react with facetious surprise, then continued. "Since we were fortunate enough to have a detective in residence during the preceding events, we have asked Sergeant Merrick of Scotland Yard to conduct the investigation. I hope all of you will do your utmost to cooperate with him."

Nickie came to the front of the room and stared coldly at us. We shivered once more, less happily. "This is a serious situation," he began ponderously. "I have determined that security is adequate at the Mimosa Inn; the gate is locked during the night and trespassers are rare, if not nonexistent, due to the distance from the highway. That leads me to conclude that the murderer is here—at the Mimosa Inn and possibly in this very room, sipping coffee or innocently buttering his or her toast!"

Several cups hit their respective saucers; triangles of toast flew across the tablecloth. We all gazed impassively at each other. The Oriental Hercule broke the silence. "Where is the deceased's wife, Sergeant Merrick? Has she been informed?"

"I've sent someone to break the news and bring her here. It is a felony to withhold information, sir. Do you have some reason to believe she's involved in this ghastly crime?"

"No, Sergeant, not at all. It's just—just that, well, she was upset at dinner, and I—I wondered—"

"I would prefer that you leave the speculation to me. That, sir, is my duty. As for the details of the crime . . . The medical examiner was called to the scene at seven-fifteen this morning, when he determined that the victim had been dead for more than six hours but less than twelve. When pressed for a more precise figure, he offered an estimate of roughly seven to nine hours."

Mrs. Robison-Dewitt had no intention of being daunted by Nickie's brusque demeanor. "The case of death, Sergeant Merrick?" she called, waving a finger in the air.

"The medical examiner has suggested the classic blunt

instrument. My men have examined all the oars and canoe paddles in the boathouse, and none of them have traces of blood or hair. I'm afraid we must search further afield for the weapon. In the meantime, I must question those of you who can assist in our inquiry."

It was as if the class had been accused of the murder. Throats were cleared; napkins were folded into precise rectangles; expressions mimicked those of a children's choir. I felt guilty, even though I knew perfectly well I hadn't bashed Harmon with anything more lethal than a frown of disapproval.

Nickie pointed toward a corner table, where Suzetta was slumped in a chair. "Miss Price, you may have been the last person to see Crundall alive. Would you please tell me what happened yesterday, from the moment of your arrival at the Mimosa Inn?"

Suzetta's face was ashen, the customary makeup absent. Her blond hair, on the other hand, had spent a considerable amount of time with a brush. She flinched as though Nickie's index finger might explode at her, then pulled herself up and said, "Harmon and I got here right after lunch yesterday. We checked in—and no matter what you think, we had separate rooms! Then he started drinking, and sort of had a teensy bit more than he could handle. I put him to bed during dinner, and didn't see him after that. I sure as hell didn't kill him!" Her voice ended on an indignant squeak.

Mimi stood in the doorway that led to the kitchen. She looked as pale and worried as her husband, but her shoulders were squared. Beneath the curtain of bangs, her eyes were flat. She would be my first choice in a crisis, I decided, despite her tendency to lapse into the ingenue role. Eric was the dreamer; she wore the pragmatic pants in the family.

"That's correct, Sergeant," she volunteered. "They did

have separate rooms, and I was the one who helped Miss Price carry Harmon Crundall to his room. He was almost unconscious by then—how did he get to the boathouse?"

"An area that requires exploration, Mrs. Vanderhan," Nickie said. "The victim was 'escorted' to his room at approximately nine o'clock last night and left to sleep off his excesses. What did you and Miss Price do, once he was safely tucked in bed?"

"I came downstairs to continue supervision of the kitchen staff, then watched the movie with our guests, Sergeant. Afterwards, Eric and I made sure that everything was locked and went to bed."

"Then you did not see Harmon Crundall once you left the room?"

"No, I did not, Sergeant Merrick."

"Miss Price?" barked Nickie, spinning around to stare at her.

"I watched the movie, too, and then went to bed."

"Did you later go by Crundall's room to see if he might need further assistance?"

Suzetta shook her head in an ash-blond flurry. "He was out like a cement block. Why would he need further assistance?"

Tugging at the end of his mustache, Nickie glared around the room. "Did any of you see or hear Crundall after he left the dining room?"

We shook our heads dumbly. At this point the door to the drawing room opened, and Bella Crundall stepped into the room. She wore a well-cut navy-blue skirt and jacket with a pastel blouse, white gloves, and a small hat, as if she had dropped by on the way to a garden club meeting. Her hair was no longer wispy, nor was her expression.

"Yes, Sergeant?" she said. "You wanted to see me?"

Nickie was startled, as were we all. After a pause, he regained his composure and said, "Did the officer inform you of the recent tragedy, Mrs. Crundall?"

"The tragedy was by no means recent; it took place thirty-one years ago when I married Harmon," she countered in a defiant tone. "I should have known that he would never change, would never repent his ways nor cease his childish cravings for liquor and women. Last night was not the first time I'd discovered him flagrantly mocking our marriage vows, but it was the last time. I told him then that I would divorce him."

"His response, Mrs. Crundall?"

"All of you heard his response. He assured me that he would try to divorce me first, and transfer his assets to his secretary's name, in order to keep me from getting my fair share." Bella found Suzetta and gave her an inscrutable look. "However, even in his drunken stupor, Harmon knew that a lawyer would be able to thwart the petty scheme. I had no reason to kill my husband, Sergeant; I had already washed my hands of him."

"Yet yesterday morning you followed him to the Mimosa Inn and attempted to register under a false name!"

"A crime, Sergeant? I think not. Yes, I followed Harmon here to confirm my suspicions. Earlier in the morning I found a notation on his desk about his reservation for the weekend, although he had told me earlier that he would be on a hunting trip with some colleagues from a distant city. He was hardly hunting squirrels."

"Mrs. Crundall, you must be frank with us."

Bella adjusted her hat, seemingly unconcerned by Nickie's increasingly dark expression. "If you're finished, I would prefer to return to my bungalow, Sergeant Merrick."

Without waiting for a reply, she left the room. Nickie gave his mustache a vicious tweak, then hurried across the room to confer with his nervous henchman. The rest of us took the opportunity to commence breathing once again. I noted the parameters of the time of death in my notebook, did a bit of subtraction on my fingers and arrived at the estimated hours: ten o'clock to midnight, when we had all been watching the movie in the drawning room.

Or had we? There had been noises in the back of the room, as if people had washed in and out on a random tide. I could vouch for my own presence the entire time, but I couldn't be sure about anyone else's, including Peter's. I looked around the room for him, and spotted him at a far table, grinning at me with an inquisitive tilt to his head. It was not worthy of response.

Nickie returned to the front of the room. "Mrs. Vanderhan, it seems that Crundall and his"—discreet cough— "secretary, Miss Price, were unaware of the special nature of the weekend. According to several witnesses, they were surprised by the whimsical plans and a bit disgruntled. If they had no reservations, why did you permit them to register?"

Mimi fluttered her hands helplessly. "Eric and I had a meeting scheduled for Monday with Mr. Crundall. He arrived Friday after lunch and announced that he had driven down early to spend a restful weekend with his secretary. Due to the nature of the meeting Monday, I could hardly refuse his demand for adjoining rooms."

"This meeting was about . . . ?"

"He had an option on some of the land surrounding the Mimosa Inn. He was a sort of—silent partner, and he wanted to discuss refinancing schemes on Monday. I had no choice."

Eric joined her in the doorway, placing one hand on her shoulder to steady her. His pipe was clenched tightly between his teeth. "That is correct, Sergeant. Harmon Crundall was a business associate, nothing more."

"Ah, Mr. Vanderhan, I have a question or two for you. If Crundall was indeed murdered during the movie last night, someone must have left the room. You were in the back of

the room with the projector; can you offer any enlighten-
ment about the group's movements?"

"It was dark," Eric said uneasily. His pipe wobbled for a
second, and he quickly stuffed it in his pocket.

"Necessarily so, in order for the movie to be visible,"
Nickie said. "Then let us return to the moment before the
lights went out. Was anyone missing from the room at that
time?"

"Mrs. Crundall did not appear, but she was in her
bungalow. I later sent Bruce down there to see if she might
want a tray from the dining room or a pot of tea."

"Bruce?"

"Bruce Wheeler, our temporary bartender. He came back
and said that Mrs. Crundall refused to answer his repeated
knocks."

Nickie scanned the room until he found the blond beach
boy, who was sitting at the table with Suzetta. "How did
you know that Mrs. Crundall was really inside the bungalow?" he barked.

Bruce carefully placed his fork on one fingertip and
balanced it with negligent confidence. "I heard her inside.
Crying. I decided not to disturb her and left."

"Did you then return to the house to watch the movie?"

The fork clattered onto the table. "I'd already seen it, so I
continued past the bungalows to walk around the lake."

Nickie digested that with a wry frown, then waved a hand
at the man poised in the doorway to the drawing room. The
man came forward with a collection of plastic bags and
arranged them on a table.

"These," Nickie said, "are the pieces of evidence found
at the scene of the crime or in Crundall's room. I will allow
you to examine them, if you wish, but they must not be
tampered with before the investigation is finished. Those of
significance will be needed at the trial."

He spun on his heel and marched out of the room. Suzetta

and Bruce followed more slowly, whispering to each other. Pale but composed, Mimi invited us to resume our meal and went into the kitchen with her husband. We sat for a decorous minute, then all shoved back our chairs and scrambled for the table with the clues. Mrs. Robison-Dewitt arrived first. Elbows primed for violence, she began sifting through the plastic bags as the rest of us advanced with caution.

Once I had worked my way through the crowd, I snatched a Baggie from under her substantial nose and studied the contents. Three long yellow threads, similiar to human hairs but with an unmistakable synthetic sheen. I dutifully recorded the information in my notebook and picked up another Baggie, labeled "victim's bedroom." Inside was a ragged corner of paper, the edges charred. I could make out a few letters: "Whereas th—" Mrs. Robison-Dewitt plucked it out of my hands, but I doubted there was anything else to be deduced from it.

A second Baggie from the bedroom contained a highball glass with a crescent of lipstick on one side of the rim, and a third a clump of mud. The last clue was from the boathouse, and was as helpful as the previous ones. I noted the matchbook (minus two matches) in my notebook and wiggled out of the crowd.

It was time to determine a game plan. Resisting the urge to dash to the boathouse to examine the scene of the crime, I forced myself to go upstairs to my room in order to contemplate the clues in peace. If Poirot could do it from his parlor, then so could Malloy.

Caron was still asleep. Dandy, I told myself as I perched on one corner of the bed and read my squiggles. The penciled message on the boathouse door still avowed that the building held the answer. It had held the body, but we all knew that. It also held dust, grime, and cobwebs, and it had held the clues Nickie left for us to examine.

I listed the suspects: Bella Crundall (for obvious reasons), Suzetta Price (for unknown reasons), Mimi and Eric Vanderhan (again, obvious reasons), Bruce Wheeler (because of his peculiar story), and Mrs. Robison-Dewitt (on principle). Five valid suspects, and one out of sheer malice. The schedule gave us until dinnertime to unravel the clues, question the suspects, and arrive at a solution.

For lack of anything else, I arranged the clues under their respective sites of discovery. Boathouse: plastic threads, matchbook. Bedroom: lipstick-smudged glass, burnt paper, piece of mud. From Nickie's comment about them, I decided that some of them might be irrelevant, not that I could find relevance in any of them. I flipped to a clean page and licked the tip of the pencil.

Harmon Crundall had come to wrest the Mimosa Inn from its devoted owners, whose protective instincts might drive them to murder. He had brought his witless secretary—except that she was by no means as witless as she acted. She had some unknown relationship with the agile bartender, who seemed to be hiding something. Bella Crundall, the estranged wife, could well be disguising her justifiable rage. Now what?

I tried a time scenario: Harmon was carried to bed at nine o'clock, after which we finished dinner and went onto the porch for brandy. Shortly after that, Mimi and Suzetta engaged in a terse conversation on the stairs, then Mimi returned to the second floor with a strained expression (and lied about it when questioned). But she couldn't have bashed Harmon and carried him to the boathouse. Harmon weighed a solid two hundred pounds, Mimi perhaps half that.

At ten o'clock we had gone inside for the movie. Bruce had been sent to check on Bella Crundall and purportedly heard her inside the bungalow. Then, according to his statement, he went for a walk. In the dark? Almost anyone could have slipped away from the drawing room, since the lights were conveniently off. Eric had seemed distressed by his inability to provide an alibi for any of us, which might indicate that he was protecting someone.

And, most interestingly of all, Suzetta had crept through the house at one-thirty and vanished in the stable area (and lied about it when questioned). To meet Bruce? To find a wheelbarrow to transport a tenth of a ton? And go thump, thump, thump down the stairs to the boathouse?

I was on a merry-go-round, making precise little circles that led precisely nowhere. I swatted Caron's exposed posterior. "Wake up, there's been a murder. I want you to help me."

An eye opened to a slit. "Why?"

So much for the hopes of a successful mother-daughter team. I changed into jeans, a knit shirt, and my Marple cardigan. Notebook in hand, I went downstairs to commence some serious sleuthing.

Peter was in front of the desk, flipping through the registration book. When he saw me, he closed the book and turned around. "Good heavens, it's the sinister spinster from St. Mary Mead. Making any progress?"

"I certainly am," I lied blithely. "There are a few loose ends to be tidied up, but I have a fairly good idea who our murderer is. How about you, Wimsey? Found any good recipes?"

"I'm sure I can find some if the need arises," he said, flashing his teeth at me. I flashed mine in response; we nodded and he strolled across the drawing room and went outside to the porch.

Once he was gone, I hurried over to the guest book and located the entries of the present guests. I had checked in about midway in the list; Harmon and Suzetta had come a few names later, after a Dr. Chong Li. Peter's name was the ultimate except for the mysterious arrival whom we now knew as Bella Crundall.

I went out the back door to explore the stable on the chance I might find a clue to Suzetta's mysterious behavior the previous night. It was a long, sturdy building, which originally had housed over a dozen horses in roomy stalls. Side walls were removed to allow cars to park under the roof. At one end there was a tack room filled with lawn mowers, bags of fertilizer, gardening tools, and odd bits of furniture in need of minor repairs. It did not seem a romantic setting for a midnight tryst, in that the dominant redolence was that of ripened organic material. I recalled Mimi's comment about the staff quarters on the second floor, and wasted a few minutes creeping up the steps to gaze at an empty, narrow hallway with closed doors.

As I started down, I saw a slip of paper tacked on a post. Giddy with optimism, I took out my pencil and prepared myself for a shattering revelation. The message read, "The blonde has an abbreviated problem of personal identity."

I stood there and reread the words approximately twenty times before I copied them into my notebook. I knew who the blonde was, and I already knew she had played a role for Harmon's and our benefit. Okay, a problem of personal identity. But abbreviated?

I heard a footstep in the tack room and ducked into a stall that housed a black Cadillac. Breathing heavily, I peeked around the bumper. Although the whole thing was a game, my heard thudded unplayfully on my stomach and my hands turned to sponges. Competition does that to me.

Mrs. Robison-Dewitt crept into view, a priggish frown on her face as she took in the wisps of straw on the floor and the cobwebs stretched across the rafters. She was heading toward the post with the clue, but I doubted it was visible from her vantage point.

I leaped to my feet and shouted, "Hello!"

It was well worth the effort. The lady turned the color of algae, shrieked, and almost lost her balance on the loose straw. Her hands were curled to battle a rapist or mugger; her expression might have sent the same into terror-stricken flight. Our eyes met across the expensive expanse of Cadillac.

"You!" she said, outraged and shrill. And brownish-green.

I opted for an innocent ploy. "Well, yes. I came out here to tighten the carburetor regulator valve on my pistons. I never thought I'd get the stubborn thing adjusted. Afterwards, I searched for clues but didn't find anything." I abruptly shifted to a solicitous expression. "Mrs. Robison-Dewitt, you're quite pale. Let me help you back to the porch to sit down. Perhaps a glass of sherry . . . ?"

She was too shocked to protest, and allowed me to lead her out of the stable and around the house to the lawn. Once we reached the porch, however, she jerked her arm free.

"Thank you, Mrs. Malloy," she said stiffly, "but I am fine. If you would be so kind as to leave me in peace, I shall soon recover."

It sounded like a promise for revenge. I gave her my sweetest smile and murmured, "But of course. Please be careful if you intend to prowl around deserted buildings; the floors can be rough."

I thought I heard her say that she could, too, but she was already through the door. Trying not to chortle, I glanced around to see what my fellow detectives were up to. The lazier (or more confident) were sunbathing near the water; the more industrious were wandering about with notebooks and guarded expressions. The boathouse had a line in front of it, as though it were a movie theater. Caron could have made a fortune selling tickets.

I strolled past the end of the line, striving to look uninterested, and continued through the garden. As I passed

the statue in the center, I heard a scraping noise. I followed
the noise to a far part of the garden, where I found Bella
Crundall on her knees in the middle of a row of roses. I
managed a timid greeting and introduced myself.

The "widow" seemed to have survived the ordeal
without any visible distress. Waving a trowel at me, she
said, "I'm a born gardener, and the sight of these neglected
roses was too much to bear. All they need is a good pruning
and a little lime worked into the soil around their roots."

"I can see that," I murmured. Limes belong in mar-
garitas. I wasn't sure what they would do for roses, but I
wasn't about to ask. Given any encouragement, avid
hobbyists can expand like hot-air balloons. "I'm sorry
about your husband, Mrs. Crundall," I added, determined
to avoid any further botanical insights.

"Call me Bella, dear." She sat back on her heels and
wiped her forehead with her sleeve. The blue suit had been
replaced with sturdy denim jeans and a flannel shirt, the
cuffs of which did little to hide the angry scratches on her
wrists. She saw me looking at them and said, "I really
shouldn't have taken it upon myself to undo years of
neglect. The bag of lime was in the tack room, but gloves
were not. My hands are already beginning to blister."

I found a grassy spot and sat down (the companionable
ploy). "The garden is rather sad, isn't it? I suppose you
noticed its condition last night when you returned to the
bungalow?"

The corners of Bella's mouth curled, but she caught
herself before she actually smiled. "Exactly, Claire. I came
back to the bungalow just as the sun was setting, and stayed
there the rest of the night. I was so distressed by
Harmon's—ah, unfortunate condition. I felt truly sorry for
the girl he was with. Thirty-one years of marriage hadn't
changed him; I doubted that she could, no matter how hard
she batted her eyelashes and flattered him."

"Did you hear Bruce knock on the door around ten o'clock?"

"I was too upset to notice much of anything, Claire. Although I fully expected to find Harmon in his disgraceful state, I was still rather shaken. So childish, pretending it was an innocent business trip." Sighing, she began to dig a small hole.

"Did you know about the option?"

"Yes," she admitted with a sigh, "and I told Harmon that he wasn't giving that nice young couple a fair chance to make a go of the Mimosa Inn. He didn't care; his heart shriveled up along with his liver. Once, when we were young and poor, I thought there might be a noble spirit under his ambition. How wrong I was . . ."

"He was a developer?" I asked encouragingly.

"He began as a real-estate salesman in a small office. By the end of five years, he owned the office and it had grown to a major operation. But Harmon was never satisfied. He not only had to make money, but also to spend it so that everyone could see how successful he was. The women were paraded so that everyone could know how virile he was. The drinking was to hide his one fear that no one would believe his ostentatious display and see through the pitiful charade."

I was impressed with the work that had gone into the weekend. It seemed that an elaborate background had been arranged for each character, and detailed stories were available for the asking. Bella's presentation had been convincing. I asked her if she had done much acting with the Farberville Community Theater.

"I'm a chemistry teacher at the high school," she answered. "I do my acting in front of a captive audience every day, and I would imagine that's more demanding than any theater presentation. The latter audience wants to be there, and they want to be amused."

That brought me back to Caron, who needed as much stimulation as a sophomore chemistry student simply to be roused from bed. I thanked Bella for talking with me and left her to dig rings aound the roses. Once at the statue, however, I followed the path that ended at the row of bungalows. Bella had moved into the first, for the shutters were pulled back and the door was slightly ajar. As tempting as it was, I could not bring myself to snoop through her room, even though I knew she was safely occupied in the rose garden.

The other two bungalows were shuttered. I pretended for a moment that I was a juggling bartender on a mission of mercy. After tapping in the direction of the door, I told myself that I heard muffled sobs and lowered my head. Now, to take a walk. I noted that the only path out of the clearing led back to the garden; the brush on the other three sides was formidable, if not impenetrable. Bruce Wheeler had not strolled onward. He had returned the way he had come . . . to meet Suzetta? No, she had been in the drawing room.

It was time to bell the cat, or at least inquire about its alibi. I turned to leave, but was suddenly aware of a prickly sensation between my shoulder blades, as though I were being tickled with a live wire. The birds had been twittering mindlessly during my visit; now they were quiet. A dry stick cracked like a finger snapping, but I could not pinpoint the direction of the sound. The sense of furtive scrutiny grew stronger and stronger, until the clearing seemed claustrophobic, the tangled undergrowth ominous.

I stared around, undoubtedly looking like a caged beast. Bella had been in the garden; had she crept up to spy on me? Or had someone followed me from the boathouse, someone who remained hidden and watchful? Unlike hardy heroines of fiction, I did not feel a swoon coming on, nor did I toy with the idea of a whining demand to know who was there.

I squared my shoulders, assumed a disdainful expression, and headed for the path through the garden. Like a sprinter with her shorts on fire, I might add.

SIX

At the edge of the garden next to the lawn, I stumbled to a halt and took a minute to catch my breath. My hair flopped over my forehead; sweat dribbled down my back in salty tears. As I patted myself into shape, I ruefully decided that my semihysterical flight had been just that: semihysterical. In retrospect, and within sight of the house, it seemed foolish at best. Gothic. Dumb, as Caron would undoubtedly giggle if she ever heard about it. The invisible watcher most likely had fur and a bushy tail, or a beak and feathers. On the other hand, talk is cheap after the fact.

Peter was beside the croquet court, watching the snail-like progress of a practice game. I tried to walk past without being noticed, but had no luck. He gave me a smile and said, "Would you like to play? I'll share my mallet with you."

"I'm busy," I snorted, continuing toward the porch.

"Still puzzled by the clues?"

"One or two of them, but I'll be ready with my solution at dinnertime," I said. I did slow down, though, and finally stopped to look back at him. "I suppose the great detective from the Farberville CID has solved the murder? Supercop strikes again and all?"

"I have a theory," he admitted with a self-deprecatory shrug that fooled me not one iota. "Why don't you practice your form—on the croquet court, of course. The tournament starts at two o'clock."

"Maybe after lunch, Peter. It takes us mortals longer to solve crimes, and I have a few people to question." I went on to the dining room to find Bruce.

He was behind the bar, cutting lemons into wedges. His hands worked so quickly that the lemons seemed to disintegrate under a flash of silver. His T-shirt did little to hide the rippling muscles of his back and upper arms, nor his jeans to disguise his gender. The boy oozed virility, sunshine, and, to my regret, youth.

When the bowl was filled, he looked up and said, "How about a Bloody Mary before lunch, Mrs. Malloy? The tabasco sauce is guaranteed to sharpen your wits."

"Then it had better be pure magic," I muttered. When the drink was prepared, I sat down at a table near the bar. "Eric said earlier that you're a temporary employee. What do you do when you're not juggling olives or making wonderful Bloody Marys?"

"I'm a grad student at Farber College. I've been in the Book Depot a few times, but we never spoke," he said, sounding as if his life were empty because of our ill-fated failure to communicate.

"What's your major?"

"Theater. I hope to combine my theatrical experience with my magic, and come up with some sort of act that will rival David Copperfield. Until my day comes, I work part-time as almost anything, including party clown, janitor, and bartender. I also chase women, although they're harder to juggle." He gave me a broad wink, the meaning of which eluded me.

He was enjoying himself too much and—I suspected—at

my expense. I decided to try the blunt ploy. "Had you ever met Miss Price before this weekend, Bruce?"

He picked up the knife and began to slice limes. "No, I saw her yesterday for the first time. What a shame for a woman like that to be hooked up with a slobbering old sot with a penchant for pinches. I saddled my white horse to rescue her from a horrible fate."

"So you were merely trying to make a pass at her?" I prodded sympathetically. "Sergeant Merrick seemed to accept your story of your actions last night with a grain of disbelief."

"The full moon, the lusty song of the bullfrogs, the whisper of the breeze in the treetops," he mused with a grin. "I was drawn by the call of the wild, Mrs. Malloy. Although Miss Price failed to join me, an animal instinct hypnotized me and led me deep into the mysterious forest."

I lifted my glass in salute to his facile response. "But weren't you dreadfully scratched by nature's mysterious thorns, Bruce? There isn't a path beyond the bungalows; I looked earlier this morning."

He put his elbows on the bar and cupped his chin in his hands to give me an impish pout. "There isn't?" When I shook my head, he added, "I must have been confused by the moonlight. I came back past the croquet court and ambled down the road to the gate."

"Alone?"

"Depressing picture, isn't it?"

"What time did nature release its hypnotic hold on you?" I asked.

"When the stars lost their sparkle, I went back to my lonely bed above the stables and cried myself to sleep. Must have been about midnight."

We studied each other for a few minutes, then Bruce went back to his preprandial preparations and I went upstairs to see what Caron was doing, if anything. To my amazement, she was not only awake, but also dressed and sitting tailor-

THE MURDER AT THE MURDER AT THE MIMOSA INN 79

fashion on the bed. As I came in, she waved a piece of paper at me.

"Another clue, Mother. It was pushed under the door this morning while I was asleep. These people have an odd way of communicating, don't they?"

"Let me see it," I said, desperate for anything, no matter how small or insignificant. On the paper was typed: "Do we have to pay? you wonder aloud as you seek the answer." I scowled at the nonsensical words. "What does it mean? Come on, dear, you're a whiz with the crosswords; figure it out for me, please."

"How should I know?" She took back the paper to glance it for a second before she let it drift to the floor. "It doesn't really matter, anyway. It's no big deal."

I caught her arm before she could drift away, too. "Listen, Caron, I realize that you have no interest in solving the murder, but it's important to me." A vision of Peter's smile came into my mind, and my fingers involuntarily tightened until Caron winced. I guiltily released her and turned on the deference. "Sorry, dear, but this is vital. Won't you please study these clues? I've never done any of those cryptic crossword puzzles, and I haven't any idea how to decipher these meaningless sentences."

Caron studied her reflection in the mirror. "How much?"

This was the weekend we were going to reestablish our relationship? I caught her watching me in the mirror and narrowed my eyes. "Five dollars a clue."

"Ten—or I'll take a nap."

"Seven-fifty or you'll take a hike, a twenty-mile hike back to Farberville. I'll personally put in an order for a thunderstorm."

"Do we include the clue I've already solved about the hobo and the boathouse?"

The girl had career potential as a union negotiator for musclebound dockworkers. The diplomatic corps was out of the question; she could provoke World War III in fifteen minutes flat. I gave her a curt nod and my notebook.

Before opening it, she assumed an air of studied casualness and said, "I may have seen something important last night, while you were watching that old movie with everyone."

"What?" I said, mentally rubbing my hands together in glee.

"I don't know if it was anything or not, but Peter Rosen seemed excited when I told him."

"You actually told that man before you told me, your own biological mother, who fed you homemade chicken soup when you had the measles and sat up all night with you when you found your first pimple? How could you do that—and why him?" Oh, the treachery!

"He asked what I did last night. He was very polite for a policeman, so I told him."

"And what precisely did you tell this paragon of civility?"

"Well," she said, lying back on the pillow with her hands entwined behind her neck, "as you know, our room overlooks the lawn and croquet court, not to mention that slime-infested fish pond."

"I am aware of the window and the pond."

"Well . . . I saw someone go across the lawn to the boathouse."

Bouncing on the bed like a chimpanzee, I shrieked, "Who?"

"It was very dark, Mother. All I saw was blond hair, but I couldn't see what color clothes or anything like that. The light from the porch just flashed on the hair for a second."

"You saw a blond-haired person leave the inn during the movie? Heading for the boathouse?"

"That's what I've been trying to tell you, Mother."

I flopped down on the other pillow and tried to absorb the new data. Suzetta, on her way to a date with Harmon

Crundall, the inn's most newsworthy corpse. He must have arranged to meet her there, although I had no good explanation why they would choose that place for a romantic interlude—or anything else. I'm a firm believer in comfort over moonlight and redolent breezes. Bedrooms are boring, but also unpopulated by animal life. Adjoining bedrooms are a snap.

From her supine position, Caron opened the notebook and held it above her nose. "The one about the abbreviated problem is obvious. Whoever this blond person may be, he or she is also a private investigator. Personal identity, abbreviated, is 'P.I.' Very obvious, Mother."

Aha, I told myself with a flutter of insight. Suzetta was not a dippy secretary; she was a private investigator hired by—hired by Mimi and Eric! Bella was conducting her own investigation; if she had hired Suzetta, there would be no reason to follow Harmon to the Mimosa Inn. Ergo, Suzetta had taken the job (and the role) in order to thwart Harmon's scheme to buy the acreage adjoining the Mimosa Inn. She must have been instructed to get the option, at any cost. But why the boathouse?

When I reiterated this to Caron, she was unimpressed. She rescued the paper from the floor, motivated by the thought of hard cash, and read, " 'Do we have to pay? you wonder aloud,' blah, blah . . . This one's simple if you follow the directions, Mother."

I snatched the paper from her. "What directions?"

"You're supposed to wonder aloud. Say 'to pay.' "

I did as ordered, and the third time it came out 'toupee.' I whooped and said, "That explains the yellow threads from the scene of the crime. Someone was wearing a toupee, which is the same thing as a wig. That means that the blonde you saw wasn't Suzetta after all!"

Caron eyed me as though I had sprouted wings and were flopping around the ceiling. "It's all quite fascinating, Mother, but you're beginning to foam about the mouth. I'm going downstairs for lunch; you might consider the wisdom of an ice pack or a tranquillizer."

"Wait a minute—what about this clue?" I demanded, scrambling through the pages to find the one that mentioned the rickety building. "What does this mean?"

Caron read it, then flashed me a sly look. "I have no idea. I'll think about it over a salad and a diet soda, however. It may come to me."

While she combed her hair and changed clothes, I pondered my theory. Someone who was not Suzetta (she would have worn a dark wig) slipped away from the drawing room to meet Harmon in the boathouse, and subsequently bashed him on the head with a blunt instrument that was not a canoe paddle.

I found the list of evidence and tried to fit each one into my theory. The burnt paper was Harmon's option, now a charred pile of ashes that had probably been flushed into eternity. The glass with lipstick on the rim meant that someone had had a drink with Harmon, and neither Eric nor Bruce was indicated. Mimi had gone back upstairs, I remembered, confirming it on my timetable. She had probably convinced Harmon to meet her for an illicit rendezvous, and warned him that they must be out of sight of the inn. Then she had disguised herself with a blond wig and gone to murder him.

Ooh, I loved it! Hugging myself smugly, I moved on to the clump of mud from the bedroom floor. It didn't fit in as well, so I dismissed it as a red herring. That left the matchbook found in the boathouse. I tried to imagine Mimi asking Harmon to strike a match so that she could take a careful aim in the dark, but that seemed less than credible.

Caron put down her brush and examined herself once more in the mirror. "Are you planning to lie there and gurgle the rest of the afternoon? I'm hungry, Mother."

"I thought you were on a diet."

"I need carbohydrates to think. You don't want me to waste away before I've finished with the clues, do you?"

I decided to take a break before returning to my brilliant solution. We went to the dining room, and once again I found myself sitting with Peter and the Oriental Hercule, who was apt to be Dr. Chong Li. To my further dismay, Mrs. Robison-Dewitt joined us minutes later. She snorted under her breath but managed to produce a chilly smile.

While everyone studied the menu, I raised an eyebrow at Peter. "So you made up a little theory about the murder? Do you think it will stand up under scrutiny, or is it just meant to amuse?"

"I see you've been talking to Caron," he said cheerfully and with unnecessary loudness. "Did she tell you about the blonde walking across the croquet court last night during the movie?"

I tried to shush him, but his words had boomed across the room. Now heads were tilted the better to hear us, my dear, and ears were aquiver. Conversations broke off in midword; no menu fluttered, no fork clattered. Silence. I felt as though I were in a television commercial for a certain stock broker.

"I'll have the chef's salad and tea!" I trilled gaily. "And lemon mousse for dessert!"

Gradually and with pained reluctance, the people at the other tables returned to their previous occupations, and I gave Peter a frozen look.

"Why did you blurt that out?" I hissed under my breath.

"It slipped out, Claire."

"It did not have to slip out at two hundred decibels." I snatched up a menu and yanked it open. Paper-clipped to one corner was another of the damnable clues. I gaped at it, then noticed Peter watching me and forced myself to scan the rest of the menu with great disinterest.

When he grew tired of smiling and looked away, I pulled the paper free and slid it to my lap to open it. It read, "Necessary to serve batter-dipped portion of minced meat, sans time limits." The daily special? A love letter from the chef? Caron could probably decipher it in half a second, but she was already giving her order to the waiter. I put it in my pocket for a later time.

Mrs. Robison-Dewitt gazed past me at Peter. "A blonde by the croquet court, you said? What time was that?"

Peter gulped as my toe connected with his shin. "I'm not sure," he said in a strained voice that gave me some satisfaction.

"About ten-thirty," Caron said absently. She turned to me and said, "Did you find a centipede in your menu, Mother? You almost jumped out of your skin."

Now I had everyone's attention again. I made a funny little noise that I hoped would pass for a laugh and said, "No, dear, I simply didn't realize that spinach quiche was on the menu. Had I noticed earlier, I might have ordered that, rather than a salad."

It went over like a three-day-old casserole. I smiled brightly until everyone at last admitted defeat and returned to their meals. Peter asked if those present were planning to play in the croquet tournament. Mrs. Robison-Dewitt leaned forward, endangering her cantilevered chest to bob her head in response. The drapery of flesh beneath her chin continued to tremble in the aftermath.

"I understand it is to be conducted with partners," she said in a honeyed voice. "Have you signed up yet, Mr. Rosen?"

"Mrs. Malloy has promised to play with me," he replied. He avoided my second kick and added, "She enjoys a bit of competition. Don't you, old girl?"

"Only when I know I'll win," I said from clenched teeth. Old girls are known for clenched teeth, real or ceramic.

When lunch was finished, Caron announced that the was going to lie out, which I presumed had nothing to do with passing out and let her go. I returned to the room and tried to fit together the various misshapen pieces of the puzzle, and arrived at a solution of sorts. Several pieces were swept under the mental carpet to await a later flash of intuitive brilliance.

Shortly before two o'clock I was feeling satisfied with what I had thus far, although I had made no progress with the message from the chef. I changed into a white sundress and a broad-brimmed straw hat (ambiance), put on my sunglasses (wrinkles), and went downstairs to knock Peter's croquet ball through a wicket, metaphorically speaking.

Eric had posted the pairings on a wide sheet of paper and drawn a complicated and incomprehensible diagram to indicate who played whom at which round. In a white suit and a bow tie, he looked quite elegant as he gave my dress a wolfish grin.

"You're dressed for the occasion, Claire. Very appropriate."

I curtsied and went to find my name on the roster. As Peter had promised, we were destined to be partners, while Mrs. Robison-Dewitt would be forced to struggle with Dr. Chong Li, who was asking Eric to kindly explain the game.

The tournament was not yet under way, so I opted to slip inside for a moment to see if Mimi was about. I found her in the kitchen, sitting on a stool and staring despondently at the empty counter. Her complexion had a waxy cast that would have enchanted Madame Tussaud.

"Mimi?" I said softly from the door.

"Oh, Claire, please come in. I was just trying to decide whether to send Bruce into town again. No matter how many lists I make, I always forget something vital. This time it's light bulbs and cucumbers."

"It must be difficult to keep up with all the details."

She sagged, then pulled herself up and smiled. "I never dreamed that running a country inn could be so complex," she said. "I was prepared for linens, menus, staff problems, and unruly guests, but that's only the beginning. Yesterday afternoon, for instance, I had a lengthy argument with the president of our county Audubon club, who makes Mrs. Robison-Dewitt sound like a harmless chickadee."

Other, less attractive birds came to mind. I was eager to establish rapport with my suspect, however, so I settled for a sympathetic murmur. "What did the woman demand?"

"She informed me that each year at this time they explore an area at the far end of the lake for grebes. I assured the woman that I had never seen a grebe, but she overruled me and announced that they would arrive at six o'clock, with binoculars, sack lunches, and nonalcoholic beverages in recyclable containers."

"That hasn't interfered with the weekend, has it? After all, we weren't able to see them this morning, much less listen to them stalk grebes," I pointed out.

"No," Mimi sighed, "it just tends to complicate things. I had to send Bruce down the road at five-forty-five to open the gate, so he wasn't available to help with the breakfast tables. One of the busboys took that as a personal affront and quit."

"Perhaps one of your other employees could help? After all, Suzetta is no longer occupied with conning Harmon Crundall."

Mimi looked at me from under the sweep of black bangs. "Very good, Claire. Yes, I hired Suzetta to see if she could get the option away from Harmon before Monday morning. That would help somewhat, since it would expire at midnight Monday and he would have to prove that we signed it last year. She took the secretarial job, although the perks were distasteful, but she couldn't manage to steal the paper. Harmon kept it in his briefcase at all times."

"Until last night," I said, "when he was too drunk to comprehend what was happening. You went back upstairs, had a drink, and invited him to meet you at the boathouse."

"I lived in New York for several years. The newspaper is filled with advice on rolling drunks, and I thought I could do it. I gave him a big sob story about Eric neglecting me and showed him where the back stairs were."

"Then you were to keep Harmon occupied until Suzetta could find his briefcase and take the document?"

"That was my plan," she admitted in a low voice, "but I chickened out at the last minute. The idea of that monster even touching me was . . . nauseating. Instead of going to the boathouse, I went for a virtuous walk."

She was lying, but I wasn't sure what part of her story was untrue. Before I could question her further, Eric stuck his head through the doorway and said, "Claire, we're ready to begin. Have you seen your partner?"

As we went outside, I told him that I hadn't seen Peter since lunch. Eric looked at his elaborate diagram and groaned. "I had this whole thing worked out, but now I'm short one pair. Dr. Chong Li has decided not to play, so if you'll be partners with—"

"Forget it, Eric. I know what you're going to say, and it is out of the question. Under no circumstance will I be partners with that—that person! As Caron would say, I'd rather eat spiders."

"But, Claire," he began, his eyes wide and imploring, "my whole diagram will collapse if I'm off two pairs. It's based on a simple negative geometric progression, and it won't come out if . . . if . . ."

"Tarantulas. Black widows. Brown recluses dipped in chocolate."

"I've already altered the diagram, and you'll only have to play two or three matches. Please?"

"You play with her."

"I can't. I'm the referee, and it wouldn't seem fair to the others."

"There's not one other soul within a mile of the Mimosa Inn who's willing to play with her?"

He shook his head mutely. I could see that he was

seconds away from falling on his knees in order to save his negative geometric progression.

"Oh, all right!" I snapped ungraciously. "Where's the damn mallet?"

A few minutes later, I found myself at one corner of the court watching Mrs. Robison-Dewitt wend her way through the wickets. Even though it looked like the silver trays would be ours, I was mentally preparing a vicious lecture for Peter, if he dared show his face. Which he did, halfway through the game.

Ignoring my glower, he took my arm and pulled me away from the court. "Harmon Crundall has been murdered," he said grimly.

"I am aware of that. How could you leave me to be partnered by Mrs. Robison-Dewitt, Peter? You know that she and I are—"

"He's dead, Claire."

I took a breath, and with what I felt to be admirable patience, said, "He is supposed to be dead; it's in the script. It would be a rather ordinary weekend if he weren't, and it would be somewhat silly of us to crawl around the boathouse floor looking for bloodstains."

"He is dead."

"And I'm Jane Marple—or Jane Fonda. You pick."

I brushed his hand off my arm and started back to the croquet court. As I did, I noticed a huddle of people at the edge of the lawn, their faces set in chalky white plaster. The binoculars draped around their necks trembled at the ends of the plastic straps. A buxom woman in a khaki safari jacket and pith helmet motioned to Peter, who gave me a helpless glance as he hurried over to join her.

I stared curiously at what I presumed was the bird-watchers' club. An icy finger danced up my spine as I took in their dazed expressions. A grebe could not be responsible for the strange stillness of the bird-watchers—no matter how peculiar its plumage, or idiosyncratic and public its mating habits.

After a whispered conversation with the woman, Peter came back to the croquet court to take Eric aside. The blood drained from Eric's face as he listened, and he began to sway with a queasy motion. The game halted, and mallets were slowly discarded. We formed a circle around Eric and Peter.

Peter took a deep breath. "Apparently, the Audubon people hiked around the lake early this morning to a nesting area they explore on an annual basis. In one of the coves they found a rowboat, and in the rowboat a body—face down in several inches of water. There was a bloody indentation on the back of his head, and no doubt about his condition. I'm sorry to have to tell you that Harmon Crundall is dead. But this time, it's no game."

SEVEN

"**P**eter disappeared inside to make telephone calls. Unwilling to break the silence or even look at one another, we stared at his back until the door slammed on his heels. The bird-watchers clearly considered us crackpots of the most dangerous variety, for they tightened their huddle and posted guards on the flank. The khaki-clad woman adjusted her helmet to a militant angle.

Blinking unhappily, Eric said, "I'd better find Mimi and let her know what happened. Perhaps some of you could round up the guests for a short announcement in the drawing room. This is—terrible, and I'm so sorry, everybody."

Mrs. Robison-Dewitt snorted. "If this is part of the staged crime, then I find it quite vulgar." When Eric shook his head mutely, she slowly rotated to peer at me, as if I were some as yet unidentified swamp thing. "Are you a part of this tasteless charade, Mrs. Malloy? You and that man who purports to be a member of the police force?"

"No, of course not," I said, perplexed. "Do you believe this is part of the pretense? The bird-watchers don't seem to be actors; they look genuinely upset. And Peter Rosen is the head of the Farberville CID. I met him during the investigation last fall."

"What sort of investigation, Mrs. Malloy?"

"A homicide," I admitted, distracted by the growing sense of uncertainty the woman had provoked. Could Peter have staged the last little drama? That would mean he had been in on the plotting the entire time, which was hard to believe. I thought back to his earlier admission that he had come to investigate an undisclosed crime. Realizing that all present, including the bird-watchers, were staring at me, I tried to adjust my halo to a winsome angle.

Mrs. Robison-Dewitt wasn't buying it. "I should have known!"

The words reverberated as she marched away. The others trailed after her, leaving me to repent my evil ways in solitude. I put my hand on my forehead and stared between my fingers at the discarded croquet mallets in the middle of the court, while I sorted through the latest mental dilemma. I ended up counting instead. There were four mallets; the other two were nowhere to be seen. Eric's toys had not been put away properly.

"You," the helmeted woman called, "come here. Have you an explanation for this peculiar situation?"

"Not a good one," I admitted. "We arrived yesterday afternoon for a murder weekend, and—"

"The murder was planned? Are you some sort of survivalist fanatics who thrive on murdering members of your organization?" She thrust her binoculars into the hands of a co-watcher. "Take these, Mr. Ruppert. I shall leave immediately to contact the Federal Bureau of Investigation! This is a sorry state of affairs, young woman, when heartless brutes are allowed to—"

"Not a real murder," I said hastily. "A make-believe murder, for fun. No one was supposed to get hurt, much less murdered."

My explanation was received with beady disbelief. "A make-believe murder? I find that hard to accept. The blood was hardly catsup, and Miss Elbertine was quite incapacitated by the discovery of the body. Her cheeks took on the color of a young loggerhead shrike and she became noticeably unsteady. We were forced to hold her head between her knees until she recovered."

Miss Elbertine nodded. "I could barely bring myself to look at the dreadful thing in the boat."

Heads began to nod in unison, like turtles bobbling in a swift current. I shrugged and left them to constrain poor Miss Elbertine from a further display of unsteadiness. Nickie Merrick joined me as I started for the house. "Did you hear about poor Crundall?" he said. "I can't believe it; everything was going so smoothly, and now . . ."

"Then it's true—and not some twist in the plot?" I demanded. The expression on his face was answer enough, and I grimly followed him into the drawing room. The guests clung together in a group; the buzz of their voices might have come from a jostled wasp nest. Indecisive, but alarmed enough to swarm.

Peter emerged from the office and went to the front of the room, where Nickie's podium still stood. He repeated what he had told the croquet group a few minutes earlier, then said, "I've contacted the Farberville CID and the county sheriff's office. The jurisdiction is being discussed now, but I have been asked to keep everyone here until someone arrives to take charge of the case."

His brisk authority convinced the last few doubters. The buzzes died, leaving an uneasy sibilance. We had come for a murder, but now that it had happened, it was less than delightful. Harmon had played a role; he was apt to have been a pleasant human being in real life. I wished I'd tried to like him better, in spite of his talented portrayal of a chauvinist sot.

Peter joined Mimi and Eric near the office, and I went over to offer whatever help I could. Mimi was on the verge of tears, her eyes magnified as if she were behind an aquarium. She gave me a humorless smile and said, "I don't think this weekend was a very good idea, do you?"

Eric patted her shoulder. "It was a good idea, honey. How could any of us know that poor old Harmon would actually . . ." His voice faded and he increased the tempo of his ineffectual pats.

Mimi suggested coffee. We went into the dining room and sat around one of the tables while the busboy put down cups and saucers. No one wanted cream or sugar; black coffee seemed befitting.

"Can you tell us any more about what happened?" I asked Peter.

"The Audubon group stumbled on the rowboat about an hour ago. According to their report, there was a delay to confirm that the corpse was indeed a corpse, and to revive fainthearted witnesses with sips of herb tea and stern admonishments to shape up. As soon as everyone was able, they rushed back to the road. I happened to run into them there, and they told me about the body."

"Why were you on the road?"

"I was taking a walk, Claire. Don't start jumping to any wild conclusions; even detectives walk once in a while."

I decided to let it go for the time being. "What about the body? Did anyone stay there with it?"

"One of the bird-watchers, who is a retired security guard. As soon as the sheriff and his squad arrive, I'll go with them to see what we can make of the scene. I don't like the situation at all; everyone has been preoccupied with the staged murder, and may have difficulty separating fantasy from fact."

"Poor Harmon," Mimi inserted with a sigh. "He was so excited about the weekend, and was already making plans for a sequel. I don't suppose he had this in mind, though."

"Then he was the instigator?" I asked Mimi.

"He is—was the director of the Community Theater and the inspiration for our murder weekend. He and his wife—" She broke off in a horror-stricken gasp. "Bella doesn't know, Eric! I'd better go find her before the sheriff arrives."

Peter murmured that he wanted to question the bird-watchers, and he and Mimi left together.

I turned to Eric. "So the Crundalls were married?"

"Harmon thought it would be easier if we played roles that were as close to reality as possible. He and Bella were married; Bruce and Suzetta are students at the college and members of the theater, and Nick Merrick is also a member. Mimi and I played ourselves, which wasn't too demanding." His fist hit the table. "I knew we shouldn't have gotten into this, but Harmon and Mimi were adamant, and I suppose everyone else went along for the experience."

"Quite an experience," Nickie commented drily from the doorway, coming in to join us. "I keep trying to convince myself that Harmon rigged the whole thing just to fool us. Set up the deal with the binocular freaks, slipped some money to the cop to act officious, and then found a cozy place to watch us all dash about in a frenzy."

"I wish," Eric groaned. He put his arms on the table and let his head sink onto them.

"Would Harmon do that?" I asked curiously.

"No, it was just a wild dream. The theater is the most important thing in his life, and he would never do anything to disrupt the show. He played Lear with a fever of one hundred and one, and went directly to the hospital when the curtain fell. Turned out to be double pneumonia; the hospital kept him for two weeks."

While I was trying to imagine Harmon in the role of Lear, Suzetta slipped into the room and closed the door behind her. "What the hell is going on?" she demanded in a tight, frightened voice.

Nickie told her what we knew. Since we knew almost nothing, it took very little time.

She sank into a chair and shoved back her hair with an angry gesture. "Is this the truth? You're not pulling some horrid practical joke, are you? He's really dead, and those people outside really found his body on the far side of the lake? That's absolutely crazy—he was supposed to be at home today! It's in the script!"

Eric lifted his head. "It's true. The sheriff and God knows who else are on the way. The reputation of the Mimosa Inn is destroyed; no one will ever stay here after all the smirky headlines. I don't know why I ever . . ." His voice dwindled once again, as though his battery had been drained by the outburst.

We sat undisturbed for what felt like a long time. Eric, Nickie, and Suzetta took turns blaming themselves for what had happened, although I failed to see how any of them could have anticipated the eerie coincidence. I finally excused myself and went to find Caron.

The drawing room was empty, the guests having gone to their rooms, I supposed. Caron was in our room, the telephone glued to her ear and her dusty shoes on the bedspread. I told her to hang up, waited out a whispered conversation that included promises of future calls, then told her what had happened.

"Murdered?" she squealed. She scrambled off the bed to drag a suitcase from under it. "I'm ready to go home—right now. This has gotten out of hand, Mother. It's one thing to creep around trying to be clever, but if people are going to start actually—"

"I am your guardian, among other things, Caron, and I am responsible for your safety. If I thought we were in danger, I would do everything possible to get away from the Mimosa Inn. However," I said, hoping she couldn't hear my nerves humming like telephone wires on Mother's Day, "we are perfectly safe."

"Sure we are. Why don't you drive the car up to the back door while I take the suitcases down the back stairs? If anyone tries to stop me, I'll tell them that I am in the throes of acute appendicitis and that you're rushing me to the emergency room for—"

"We cannot leave until we have been questioned, dear. You'll have to accept that. This is a real investigation, and we're involved—whether we like it or not."

"Peter will let us leave," she pleaded, tossing clothes into her suitcase with the force of a bulldozer. "Give me ten minutes, Mother, and then we can just sneak out the back door to the car and drive away. It'll work."

"It won't work. For one thing, Peter is not in charge of the investigation, and if he were, he wouldn't let us leave the Mimosa Inn if we were on the verge of starvation."

"He'd let you walk on his face if you'd stop glowering at him all the time."

I narrowed my eyes and switched on the maternal frown. "You are babbling, which I find unattractive. After you change into something suitable, we will return to the drawing room to wait. And we will not discuss Peter Rosen, under any circumstances. You do not understand the man any more than you understand an existence that excludes chlorinated water."

Switching on the adolescent scowl, Caron slung the last of her clothes in a suitcase, sat on it to force it closed, and banged the lock with her fist. I sat on the bed and tried to picture Harmon's body in a rowboat across the lake. How long had he been dead? And who could have rowed the boat to a distant cove?

Almost anyone, I concluded. Very creepy.

A siren grew louder, accompanied by a drone of car engines. The shrill noise peaked, then died in a spiraling whine. Car doors slammed, voices shouted orders and counterorders, and feet thudded across the floor downstairs.

The sheriff, his posse, and possibly a battalion of marines had arrived.

Caron picked up the telephone receiver. "I am going to call Inez. I need to maintain contact with the outside world; otherwise I'll end up as crazy as the rest of you!"

"The rest of you" referred to, I suspected, that generation of people older than fourteen years of age. Wondering if she had a valid point, I returned to the drawing room to find out what was to happen.

The sheriff was issuing instructions to a bevy of scurrying minions, all dressed in trim beige uniforms and brimmed hats. The sheriff was similarly dressed, but the effect was less than impressive. I had expected a cartoon version of a rural lawman; the reality was a contradiction of the stereotype. He was a slight man, clean-shaven, with short dark hair and wire rimmed glasses. No bulldog jaw or expanse of girth. His overall appearance was that of an accountant hired to find a pesky error in the books.

"You're—ah, Claire Malloy?" a deputy asked, stopping me at the foot of the stairs. "You're here with your daughter Caron?"

I was ticked off on his list and sent to wait until the sheriff could talk to us as a group. My comrades drifted in as I had done, were asked their names, and then sent on to the drawing room. Dr. Chong Li tried a few questions, but was rebuffed with officious curtness. Not even Mrs. Robison-Dewitt could elicit any information, despite her threat to write an exposé on police insensitivity in the *Ozark Chronicle*.

There must have been a reason to keep us sitting for over two hours, but it eluded me, as well as the others. Conversation seemed inappropriate; thinking, however, led to unpleasant images and a lot of chewed fingernails. I caught myself wishing *I* were upstairs on the telephone with Inez, although I might have run out of topics as the hours crept by. Caron and Inez would be strong contenders in a telephone marathon; their endurance was incredible.

Just at the point when rebellion was imminent, Peter and the sheriff came into the room. The sheriff took off his hat to wipe a veneer of sweat off his forehead, then said, "Several of my deputies are still at the crime scene, but we have completed the initial investigation."

Déjà vu to the max, as Caron would say. From the shifting of bodies around me, I sensed that I was not the only one in the room reliving the moment in the dining room earlier, when Nickie Merrick had begun in the same way. Then it had been fun and games—a major difference.

"I have had a long discussion with the authorities both in Farberville and in my office, and we have decided that Lieutenant Rosen will take charge of the investigation," the sheriff continued in a mild voice. "Although his jurisdiction is limited to Farbeville, he has been present since Friday afternoon and seems the logical choice. My men and I will remain to offer assistance."

Peter gave us a bemused look as he stepped forward. "Strange, isn't it? But we'll all have to forget about the game and get on with the more serious problem so that we can go home." He waited out a rumble of displeasure at the implicit warning that we might not be permitted to have brunch and toddle away in the morning. "Unlike our man from Scotland Yard, I am not going to publicly question the suspects and pass out the clues. I will see you one at a time, in the office near the back door. If in your sleuthing you saw anything at all that seemed incongruous, please tell me; in the meantime, you may return to your rooms or use the facilities of the inn."

Mrs. Robison-Dewitt lifted a finger. "We know nothing of what has happened to Mr. Crundall. Therefore we have no way to determine what may or may not be congruent to your investigation, Lieutenant Rosen." She managed to make his name an insult. I wondered if she still suspected

Harmon would at any moment leap out of a closet to chortle at us. He would receive a chilly reception.

"Then perhaps you'd care to be the first to join me in the office?" Peter said levelly. Above his jutting nose, his eyes glinted with anger, but he managed to maintain a civil expression. "I'll see the rest of you over the next few hours. Please remain available until your statement has been taken."

School was dismissed. Although I was gripped by curiosity, I was not about to ask Peter any questions until my name floated to the top of his hit list. I finally decided to make an exit before I was coerced into speculation, and went across the lawn and through the garden. Mimi had not reappeared; I presumed she was still with Bella at the bungalow. I hurried through the garden.

Mimi met me at the door of the bungalow. "I'm glad you came, Claire. There are a million things I need to do, but I hated to leave Bella alone, even for a few minutes. The press will probably arrive in a herd, and we will have to serve dinner. Is everybody fairly—did the sheriff—oh, this is terrible! I don't know if I can deal with it, Claire!"

I made encouraging noises and sent her back to the inn to face a crowd of distressed guests, inflated deputies, sulky staff, and whatever else she would encounter. Consoling Bella was infinitely easier, I thought, as I went into the bungalow.

Bella lay on the sofa, her face hidden under a compress fashioned out of a washcloth. She lifted one corner at the sound of my footsteps and said, "Claire, how kind of you to come."

"I didn't know if there was anything I could do, but I wanted to come," I said, studying her grayish face for signs of an impending breakdown. Bella's demeanor might have alarmed a doctor, but she seemed fairly composed. I suggested tea and busied myself in the narrow kitchen for a few minutes, then brought her a cup laced with brandy from a cabinet.

I offered my sympathies, then added, "All the guests are bewildered by the parallel events. We feel we're reliving a scene from a previous life."

"Mimi's in a state of shock, poor girl. She kept repeating that it was all her fault for ever suggesting the mock murder, and looking as though she might start beating her breast and ripping out her hair in penance. She's more upset than I am, although I suspect in my case the truth hasn't sunk in yet."

"Was it Mimi's idea?"

"It was more Harmon's idea, I'm afraid. He attended one of these weekends on a trip to New York last fall, and decided it was a wonderful project for our theater group. Once Harmon shoved a bee in his bonnet, an acre of clover couldn't lure it out."

"Then he introduced the idea to the theater and did the plot?" I asked.

"I don't know who actually devised the plot," Bella said. "I was busy with midterm grades at the time, and couldn't attend the brain-storming sessions at the theater. Harmon thought it would be more amusing for us if we had no idea what the others were doing. We did go over some of the scenes together, but each of us was aware only of his or her own schedule, except when it coincided with someone else's. Harmon had the only master, I believe. Would you like to see mine?"

Bella took a typed page from her suitcast and showed it to me. She had followed her directions well, showing up at the designated time to create the scene in the drawing room, then reappearing at both dinner and breakfast. A few notes were scribbled in the margins, but the directions were downright terse.

"No one wrote any dialogue?" I said, perplexed by the skimpiness of her script.

"Harmon felt that we ought to improvise the scenes as we

went along, so that we would sound more spontaneous. We had precise times and explanatory material to be introduced, but we were on our own with the actual lines."

"It was convincing," I admitted. "I kept trying to figure out which of you were players and which were genuine money-paying guests. Your initial entrance was remarkable."

"I was glad you were there to see it, Claire, and I enjoyed feeding you the story in the garden. Although I'm sure it wasn't terribly ethical of me, I was rooting for you to solve the mystery . . . when it was a game." She lowered her eyes and sighed.

"Now that the game has been canceled, can you tell me about the clues and all?" Not terribly ethical of me, either.

"Harmon mentioned that he was writing some cryptic little messages to be salted around the scene, but I have no idea what they were. Frankly, I didn't care. I spend enough time with childish pastimes during the week, and I was not enchanted with the idea of using a weekend for more of the same."

"Then you are a high-school teacher, as you told me earlier? Was Harmon really a developer, or was that fiction?"

"He was a developer, and the first part of the story was basically true. However, our marriage was fine and he was not the womanizing monster I made him out to be. His major interest in life was the theater. I hoped we could travel once he retired, but he auditioned for a minor role, was chosen, and promptly fell in love with acting. Almost every night and weekend he was at the theater, directing or playing a role. He was the patron saint of the Farberville Community Theater, and the angel for most of the productions."

"Angel?" I echoed blankly. It seemed extreme.

"It's a theater term for the backer, the one who finances the production. Although the group is sincere and dedicated, the house receipts rarely pay the utility bills. Harmon felt needed, which was important to him."

"How did Mimi fit in with the group?"

"She was our leading lady," Bella said. "Harmon met her when the Vanderhans bought the inn, and learned that she had some experience on Broadway. No name in lights or anything like that, but small parts in real shows. Harmon was absolutely enchanted, and he insisted that she join the troupe. He even persuaded Eric to help with the sets."

"She was quite good in her role," I said. "I have her in my notebook as the most likely murderer—oh, I'm sorry, Bella. I didn't intend to . . ." I could almost taste crepe soles in my mouth.

"Don't worry about it. Harmon chose a most complicated time to be murdered, and I accept the fact that everyone is apt to confuse the two events," Bella said, with more grace than I could have produced in a similar situation. "I just wish I knew when the curtain will drop on the second act of the play. I force myself to think about my flower beds at home, and about the mundane details that will occupy me. But I can't do anything about a funeral until the body has been released, nor can I find the strength to notify relatives and close friends."

She sank back, suddenly exhausted and old. I offered to call someone for her, but she shook her head. I refilled her teacup and left her to sleep.

I stopped in the garden next to the cherub, wondering how the day could be so pretty when it ought to be dreary and cold. The birds were cheery, the sky cloudless, the leaves on the trees and shrubs bright with pastel clarity. The cherub seemed pleased with his one-footed pose, and optimistic that at some point the water would once again dribble down to the leaf-filled basin beneath him.

I sat down on a bench to consider what had happened. That took about fifteen seconds, so I moved on to what I had learned about the theater troupe. No startling insights there;

everyone was involved with an undemanding role. Husbands, wives, students. Harmon and Suzetta had been assigned the most difficult roles, but they had deported themselves well. Harmon had carried his role to a fatal conclusion, however.

My noisy sigh sent a bluejay flapping away with an angry squawk. Could the murderer have come from the outside? Nickie had told us that the gate was locked, but that might have been scripted. What we needed was a psychotic drifter who had seen the sign from the highway and drifted in to find food or money. He would have been more than a little crazy to row a boat across the lake, I concluded morosely. A bona fide drifter would have quietly drifted away, unconcerned by the aftermath of the crime.

I discarded the fantasy and tried for a more prosaic analysis. I mentally went over the time scenario I had written in my notebook, hoping I might be able to spot any movement that was not a part of the script. A clump of little gray matter expired without any success. But, I thought with a flicker of excitement, each player had only his or her schedule of appearances and confrontations, so none of them would be able to recognize a discrepancy in the plot any more than I could. If I could get my hands on the master script, then I could compare it to what I had in my notebook.

A vague return of the competitive spirit sent me to my feet. All I needed to do was to ask Mimi to locate the script, then take it away to study it. Peter could plod along with his fingerprint kit and tedious questions, while I solved the murder by sheer intuitive brilliance. Again.

A deputy stumbled into view and glared at me as if I'd taken an unauthorized recess. "Mrs. Malloy?" he panted, trying to sound ominous despite his ungainly entrance. "Lieutenant Rosen has been asking for you for over thirty minutes. You're supposed to have kept yourself available for questioning."

"A crime, Sergeant? I think not," I retorted coldly.

He stiffened. "I'm a corporal, ma'am."

I held out my wrists to invite handcuffs. "Drag me to the interrogation room, Corporal. But I will not talk, no matter how tight the thumbscrews. I have concealed a cyanide tablet on my body. Rather than betray my compatriots, I shall die first!"

There was no excuse to behave like that, and I should have apologized immediately and offered some excuse about the heat. Nevertheless, I lifted my chin resolutely and marched out of the garden toward the Mimosa Inn and the firing squad—as soon as someone lined one up. The deputy puffed along behind me, muttering words best left unspecified.

EIGHT

"I hope you don't have any crazy ideas about trying to solve this homicide," Peter said as I came into the office. "There is no champagne for the winner, nor is there any gourmet dinner. The game is over, Claire. I want you to keep your nose out of the investigation."

Inwardly, I was less than warmed by the reception, but I pasted on a meek expression and said, "Of course not. I would never dream of interfering in a police investigation."

"Why do I have such difficulty believing you?"

I did not tell him that his instincts were good. Instead, I settled for a martyred sigh, meant to convey how deeply he had wounded me with his callous remark. "I have no intention of involving myself in Harmon Crundall's death. What time was he killed, by the way?"

"The medical examiner estimated the time of death to be between ten o'clock and midnight. Once he's completed the autopsy, he'll have an official report, but we're presuming that the death coincided with the staged time."

"A charming coincidence," I murmured.

Peter sat back and ran a hand through his dark curly hair.

"This whole thing is going to drive me crazy. The script was written so that any of the actors could be the villian in the story, and so, of course, not one of the actors has an alibi. A darkened room with people moving about; the boathouse conveniently placed out of the light from the porch; motives abounding but not necessarily real."

"Have you finished with the statements?"

"I've seen most of the guests, and all of the troupe except for Bella Crundall, although I don't expect to hear anything of value. Thus far I've heard the same story from everyone. The actors claim it was all a big shock, no reason for anyone to murder Crundall, a happy family of amateur actors presenting a weekend of fashionable entertainment."

"How about the guests, then? Perhaps someone was nursing a grudge from a business deal, or is a closet maniac who got carried away with the ambiance."

"Mrs. Robison-Dewitt had an identical theory. Guess whom she mentioned as the most likely maniac?"

"I don't suppose she happened to leave the drawing room during the movie, a baseball bat in one hand?"

"You'll have to discuss that with her. Now tell me what you saw and did from your arrival at noon yesterday."

I dutifully told him of all my excursions and of the clues I had found in various places. I saw no reason to mention that Caron was the one who deciphered the cryptic clues, and I omitted my mental ramblings on general principle.

Peter jotted things down during my narrative, then flashed his teeth at me and told me that I was excused. Although I expected a stern word of warning as I left, he waved me out and began to reread my statement.

Caron was sitting on a settee in the drawing room, her lower lip extended to its utmost. "That man"—glaring at a deputy—"came to our room and made me come down-stairs. I thought the Gestapo was disbanded at the end of World War II."

"That's the current theory," I said. "Have you had your turn in the office?"

"No, I have been sitting on this lumpy thing for hours and hours, with nothing to do but stare at the wall. I didn't pay any attention to what's been going on, Mother. I fail to see why I, a mere child, should be interrogated as if I were a common criminal."

The deputy edged closer, perhaps planning to thwart an escape attempt. From his expression (not warm), it was clear that Caron had already expounded on her self-righteous outrage for him, several times.

I gave her a stern look. "If you, a mere child, have seen nothing of interest, then I presume your interrogation will be brief. I'll meet you on the porch."

"I ought to call the American Civil Liberties Union," she growled with a contemptuous sniff for her neo-Nazi jailer.

"If you decide to do so, please make it a collect call." I left her to fume in chintzy solitude and went through the dining room to the kitchen to see if Mimi was there.

As I put my hand on the door, I heard a muffled sob. It was followed by a series of sympathetic noises meant to be comforting. Eric and Mimi, I realized as I let my hand fall back. I had no desire to interrupt a private conversation. On the other hand, the meek are going to have to wait a long time to realize their smog-ridden inheritance. I tilted my head and leaned forward.

"Oh, Eric," Mimi wailed, "I just cannot bear all this—this guilt! It's not my fault that Harmon insisted on doing the murder weekend. I told him that it was nonsense, but I could hardly refuse, since he . . ."

"Of course not, honey. Harmon—well, Harmon was Harmon. When he insisted, we had to let him go ahead with the crazy idea. After all, he was . . ."

"What happens now?" Mimi wavered. "Now that he's dead, does that mean that the . . . ?"

"We'll have to consult a lawyer, but . . ."

"Do you think that we can . . . ?"

Neither seemed capable of completing a sentence. I had to restrain myself from shoving open the door to demand a satisfactory amount of closure, since it might have been misconstrued as snooping. Eavesdroppers have limited rights. I was frantic to know what the obscure references were about, although Harmon's death seemed the focal point. Something legal, clearly, and under question in light of the current (postmortem) situation.

I realized that the disjointed conversation was over, and that I was apt to be caught in my undignified position if I lingered to brood. I tapped on the door and went in.

"Mimi?" I chirped brightly.

Eric stood in front of the oversized freezer. Despite his attempt to look unconcerned, his eyes flickered with a yellowish fever behind his thick lenses. Across the room, Mimi clutched the edge of the sink, her shoulders hunched and trembling as she gave me a smile intended to convey pleasure at my untimely entrance.

"Claire, I thought you were with Bella. Is there something she needs? Perhaps a pot of tea, or something to eat?"

I told her that Bella was, I hoped, napping for the moment and agreed to take a tray later in the afternoon. After a moment of silence, Eric mumbled something about the guests and abandoned the ship with ratlike haste.

Mimi took a deep breath. "Is there something else, Claire? I was about to see to the dinner menu, and the kitchen help will be here in a minute or two. It seems that murder does not preclude hunger."

She reminded me of a little girl dressed in her mother's clothes, although she was hardly tottering on high heels. The violet eyes were wary under the curtain of bangs, and the mouth was set in a stubborn line. I opted for a cautious approach.

"Have you finished with Peter, then? Did he offer any hope that this mess would be settled quickly?"

"No," she said, "he implied that we were in for a long investigation. He seems to think that the murderer is one of the people staying at the inn, since the padlock on the gate is adequate to keep out trespassers and tourists during the night. Our security is too good, if such a thing is possible. But why would anyone . . . ?"

"Then you can't think of any motive for someone to murder Harmon? Surely he's been in a few business deals that have left bad feelings, or stepped on someone's toes along the way."

"Harmon was a wonderful man. He kept the theater going despite all sorts of financial woes, and was even talking about securing a mortgage on a new building for us. And, of course, he was a saint to take the option last fall so that we could buy the inn."

"There really was an option? I thought that was simply a bit of the script."

Mimi looked dismayed by the inadvertent candidness of her character reference. "Well, it wasn't common knowledge," she said sulkily. "Harmon decided to utilize it in the script to provide a few motives, but he assured us months ago he had no intention of ever exercising it. He said he wasn't interested in doing any more developments. In fact, he said he would let Suzetta burn the actual paper when she found it in his room."

"Did she?"

"I suppose so. If there's nothing else, I need to see about dinner, Claire. The staff are as upset as the rest of us, and I must calm them down so that we can deal with necessities."

"Yes, actually there is something else," I said. "Bella told me that Harmon had the master script. Since the game is over, I'd like to see it in order to find out how I did as a sleuth. Do you know where it is?"

"We were using my office as a war room, so I would guess it's in there somewhere," she said with a shrug. "I don't see any reason why you shouldn't look at it. Now I really must get organized so that the staff can begin dinner."

I wandered out of the kitchen obediently, but I did not dash to the office to search for the master script. Not with Peter behind the desk. Later, I told myself, as I went through the vacant drawing room to the porch to see if Caron had survived the interrogation without any permanent damage to her fragile psyche.

The guests were milling about like a herd of sheep attended by a lupine, undernourished shepherd. Several uniformed officers were trying to seem unobtrusive as they hovered. Bruce was doing a steady business behind the portable bar, and from a corner Mrs. Robison-Dewitt watched me with an icy frown, no doubt eager for some symptom of madness to surface so that she could point an accusatory finger at me. I left her with her dreams and joined Caron on the top step. She seemed intact, or at least superficially so.

"Did Peter have to resort to torture?" I asked. The only response I received was a croak.

Beyond the sloping lawn, the lake rippled in a soft breeze, as serene as a puddle after a summer storm. A deceptive tranquility, I decided, as I searched the far shore for a sign of police activity. Somewhere across the brown-gray surface, a rowboat had been abandoned in a cove, its sole passenger unable to complain about the finality of the one-way trip. I wondered if the selection of the cove might have some significance.

I gave Caron a poke. "Let's take a hike before dinner," I suggested in the hearty voice of a scout leader.

"As in walk? You must be kidding, Mother. For one thing, I am exhausted by the session in the star chamber, and for another, I see no reason to voluntarily expose myself to chiggers, snakes, ticks, spiders, mosquitoes—"

"On your feet. The exercise will do wonders for your diet, and the change of scenery will do wonders for my frame of mind. If you will not come with me, I will have Eric remove the telephone from our room and you can spend the remainder of the weekend swimming—in the lake."

The envisioned horror was adequate to force her to her feet. We strolled across the lawn and down the road toward the gate. Caron lagged behind, emitting low noises, but refrained from vocalizing herself into a cordless, fish-filled existence.

Once we were a fair distance from the Inn, I began to study the brush for some sort of path that would take us around the far side of the lake, where I might find some clue to the location of the crime scene. Caron had no problem unraveling my intent, and her face took on a hostile glaze.

"I am not about to walk in the woods," she said, hugging her shoulders as if the spiders were already choosing the best freckles for dinner. "I am allergic."

"You are not allergic to anything," I said firmly. I glared her back into step, then cautiously pushed through a clump of weeds to examine a cleared patch of ground. "Is this an old logging trail? Look, there are tire marks in the dust and a cigarette butt."

"Fascinating. If we're lucky, we may see dead leaves and rocks, too. Mother, let's go back before some creepy something comes out from under a log."

"This is the only break in the brush, so it must be the trail the Audubon people used. If I'm right, it'll lead us to the cove where they found the rowboat. I don't know if we'll be able to tell where they stopped, but if we—"

"Take the telephone!"

Before I could respond, she marched back up the road to the Mimosa Inn, her lower lip pointing the way more precisely than a highway sign. Puffs of dust rose from her heels.

I swore under my breath as I watched her disappear around a curve in the road. I waited a few seconds on the off chance she might return, then resolutely turned back to the overgrown road that disappeared into the woods.

It was nearly six o'clock by now, and the sunlight had shifted to a curious, golden glow that made the woods resemble a movie set, a place where lions sang and hirsute people swung on vines. The birds had gone home, but the insects were very much in attendance. Two hours until sunset, I told myself with the confidence of someone who might be able to find the cove and be back on the road before darkness set in.

With a deep breath, I forged into the wilderness.

Ten minutes later, I began to sense the extent of my folly. The logging trail dwindled to an unkempt path that threatened to quit at any moment. Although the lake lay to my left, the trail wandered up the side of the mountain, joined a rocky stream bed for what seemed like a mile, and only then began a gradual descent. In the meantime, I had an entourage of nasty little gnats that hovered about my face in a carnivorous cloud. My arms were covered with scratches, my face with bug bites, and the rest of me with sweat. All so I could possibly find a cove that had already been examined by professionals for the most minute of clues.

I made a few comments to Mother Nature about her lack of hospitality, and a few more to the sun that was diving earthward with unnecessary haste. By now I suspected I had no more than an hour to get back to the road, unless I wanted to rely on my Daniel Boone instincts—that fell somewhere between nil and nonexistent.

Abruptly, I found the lake, which was no great feat but at least let me glimpse civilization in the distance. The Mimosa Inn looked as welcoming as a stiff drink after a session in the salt mines, and the scattered boats on the lake as comforting as a fellow tourist in Katmandu. But I was on a mission, no matter how foolish it now seemed. I wrenched my eyes back to business.

The path clung to the edge of the lake, and the foliage thinned out enough for me to walk at a reasonable pace. Where the hell was the cove?

Coves are pretty much the same after you've studied a few of them. Mud, swarms of insects, slippery moss, and the aroma of dead fish. Beached tadpoles, baked to shriveled silver ribbons. Unseen things that plopped away, or rustled in the leaves. Occasional footprints in the mud, where the Audubons had halted to search for grebes. The omnipresent rusty beer cans that both Edmund Hillary and Admiral Byrd had undoubtedly found at the ends of their respective trips.

I promised myself one final cove before giving up. The path, now a dear and trusted friend, twisted inland briefly and then abruptly spewed me out into a cleared area. The Cove, my personal grail. How could I be sure? It was no problem at all, because Peter Rosen was sitting on a log beside the water—smiling at me. A motorboat bobbed a few feet from the muddy shore.

He politely stood up as I slipped across the mud. "Did you have a nice hike, Claire?"

"I had a lovely hike, thank you. I must have seen a dozen grebes, not to mention other specimens of nature," I said, grinding my teeth into a semblance of a smile. "What are you doing here?"

"I came to watch the sunset. Will you join me? I'm afraid the sofa is a bit dirty, but the view will be spectacular."

"Have you been here long?" I asked as I accepted the inevitability of the situation and sat down beside him.

"A few minutes. I happened to notice Caron staggering up the road, and she offered the information that you felt some desire to commune with nature. She did not feel the same desire, apparently, and was more interested in making a telephone call."

"A loquacious child. I never should have encouraged her to learn to talk. What other information was she compelled to offer?"

"She did mention something about your destination."

I hoped Caron was enjoying her final telephone conversation. It would have to suffice until high-school graduation. I took off my shoe to examine a blister, studied the ring of bites around my ankle, and eased the shoe back on with a faint groan.

"May I hitch a ride back with you in the boat? I don't think I can walk more than three steps."

Peter gave me the benefit of his choirboy smile. "It would be almost impossible to follow the trail in the dark, wouldn't it? A person might sprain an ankle, or trip over some invisible rock and break a leg. It might be better to wait until morning—except for the bears. They mate in the early summer—and I understand they have foul tempers. The courtship process, I believe."

"There are no bears in the woods." After the last hour in the woods, I felt as knowledgeable as Ranger Rick.

"Probably not," he agreed graciously. "The skunks keep them away. There are skunks all over the woods."

"There are skunks around here; I can smell something in the air. I would appreciate a ride back in the boat. However, if you are going to sit here and play silly, infantile games, then I am quite capable of hiking back to the road."

The bantering tone was gone as he said, "You promised to stay out of the investigation, Claire. There is no longer an actor with a clever script—there is a cold-blooded murderer who might kill again if cornered. I thought I could trust you this time, but I was wrong."

He would have made a dandy elementary-school principal. Pain in his voice, coupled with a basset-houndish look of disappointment. Little Claire, on the carpet, given one last chance to save herself from disgrace. I preferred my chances with the skunks.

"I just wanted to see the scene of the crime," I said in a low apologetic voice. "But if you're going to fuss, I won't even look around. As soon as I'm in the boat, I'll close my eyes and not peek until we're across the lake."

"Claire." It came out in a whoosh of discouragement.

"If you insist, I'll close my eyes right now and feel my way to the boat."

"This is not a game, dammit! I wish you'd realize that and stop trying to out-sleuth me. Just let me do my job so that we can all go home before next winter."

"If I let you do your job, we might be here to count the daffodils!" I snapped. "I do not enjoy being treated as if I were some sort of egotistical busybody, Peter Rosen. I happen to know quite a bit of information that could be helpful, but you won't even listen to me, much less treat me like an adult!" A wonderful display of self-control and maturity.

"What do you know that might be helpful?"

"I'm not going to tell you!"

It was insane. We glowered at each other, hands clenched, faces red, eyes flickering like sparklers. At that moment, I would have cheerfully shoved him over backwards, hopped in the boat, and left him to hike back to the road—with the bears, skunks, snakes, and anything else silly enough to tackle him. The next moment we were wrapped around each other and behaving in a very adult manner.

It lasted a long while, and was quite pleasant despite my inner state of shock. Peter seemed adept at what he was doing. I seemed adept at what I was doing. We made a cooperative team. Finally, when I was beginning to need a breath, I unwrapped myself and eased away.

"Oh, dear," I said, flicking a gnat off my knee.

Peter raised an eyebrow. "Oh, dear? Is that all you can say?"

"What should I say in this situation—thank you?"

"I suppose not," he said. He, too, found a gnat to send away in a terminal arc.

I will not go into my personal feelings, beyond a mild comparison to those experienced by the heroine of a gothic novel who has discovered that the wretched man is not an embezzler or her first cousin or whatever she inevitably discovers in Chapter Nine-and-a-half, so that the graphic grappling can follow in Chapter Ten. On the other hand, I was hardly a nineteen-year-old orphaned virgin adrift in a heartless world. Caron is not so easily ignored.

We sat in silence for a few minutes. I toyed with a few sentences, but rejected them for triteness, gushiness, and various adolescent tinges. The only thing to do was to ignore it, I decided at last.

Watching him out of the corner of my eye, I said, "I might fill in a few omissions in my statement, if you're willing to reciprocate."

"I suppose it wouldn't hurt to discuss the case, but I want a sincere promise that you won't pull any stunts. You have a dinner to cook—for me, remember?"

"Oh, really? Then you had already solved the mock murder? Or did you find the master script in the office and happen to glance over it out of idle curiosity?"

"There was no script in the office; I searched every inch of it. But, yes, I had arrived at a solution by noon today. All those years of stodgy police work, perhaps. How did you do?"

"I do have a solution for the mock murder, but I thought we were going to discuss the real one. Is this the cove where the rowboat was found? I don't suppose there were any telltale footsteps in the mud, or fingerprints in the oars?"

"The bird-watchers trampled out any footsteps," Peter said with a grimace, "and oars do not take fingerprints. The boat has been taken in for examination, but I doubt we'll learn anything useful. Someone went to a lot of trouble to bring the body all the way across the lake. He or she wouldn't be so polite as to leave a business card in the bottom of the boat."

"He or she? You don't honestly believe a woman could be involved, do you?"

Peter studied the mud. "The sheriff is pushing for an arrest before evening. He seems to think that we have a fairly good case, although much of it is circumstantial."

"A fairly good case?" I echoed, surprised. I realized that he was avoiding my eyes. "Who?"

"Mimi Vanderhan," he admitted in a low voice. "She freely admitted that she met Harmon in the boathouse, as scheduled. According to her story, they talked for a few minutes about how successful the weekend was, and then she went to her room before returning to catch the last few minutes of the movie. However, Eric was supposed to have confronted Harmon immediately after she left—and he swears that Harmon wasn't there."

"So Harmon left the boathouse. That's not too impossible to accept, is it? Maybe someone else came by and lured him away," I pointed out with unassailable logic.

"In the space of two or three minutes? Eric was already on the porch, and he would have seen Harmon and this fancied visitor leaving together. The sheriff has a good argument, Claire. Harmon was in the boathouse with Mimi at ten-thirty, and was not there at ten-thirty-five when Eric arrived."

"Does the sheriff think that Mimi carried Harmon away on her back, or merely waved a magic wand and turned him into a spider?"

"The sheriff thinks that Mimi clouted him with something so that his body fell into a boat. She then tossed a tarp over it, left the boathouse as scheduled, and later returned to transport the gruesome cargo over here."

"But why?" I protested, wincing as I remembered Eric's childlike devotion to his wife. "She doesn't have a motive, Peter. Earlier this afternoon, she told me that Harmon was the patron saint of the Farberville Community Theater. He was going to purchase a new building for the theater."

Peter shook his head. "Bella Crundall gave me a rather different version of the relationship. She said that Harmon had an option on about three hundred acres next to the inn, and that Mimi and Eric had been frantic to buy it back from him. But he was interested in putting in a vast development called, if you can stomach it, Harmony Hills. The inn would be a joke, sitting beside suburbia."

"Mimi said that Harmon wasn't going to exercise the option, that he planned to allow it to expire quietly. In fact, he told Mimi that it would be a prop in the scenario and would end up a charred pile of ashes. One corner of it was presented in a Baggie this morning."

"No, Suzetta Price said that the paper she burned was a blank contract. Bella was adamant about the fact that Harmon intended to exercise the option despite the Vanderhans' pleas. It was a very lucrative deal for him. Several hundred thousand dollars, minimum."

"Well, I refuse to believe that Mimi would murder anyone, much less Harmon! Your sheriff has the mind of a gnat. Mimi is a nice person, and she wouldn't bash Harmon."

"I don't like it, either," Peter said, offering a hand to pull me to my feet. "But Mimi may be in custody by the time we get across the lake, so you'd better be prepared."

"I'll be prepared," I vowed in a cold voice as the mud sucked at the bottoms of my shoes. "But the sheriff had better be prepared, too!"

NINE

The sheriff was waiting for us on the grassy beach in front of the inn. Behind him, Eric stood unmoving, his demeanor as lively as that of a cigar-store Indian. On the porch the guests had gathered to watch the latest scene.

"Ah, Rosen, I need to discuss something with you," the sheriff murmured. They moved away to talk in terse whispers. Peter shook his head several times, but the sheriff continued steadily until at last they seemed to reach an agreement, albeit tentative on one side.

I hurried across the grass to shake Eric's arm. "Where's Mimi?" I demanded in my own terse whisper.

"They—they put her in a police car. Claire, they seem to think that she—that she was the one who . . . Mimi didn't murder Harmon. She wouldn't hurt anyone, and she thought Harmon was a wonderful man. I suppose I ought to do something, but I—"

He clamped his lips together and blinked several times. His Adam's apple rippled in his throat as if it were on a elastic string. "I was the one who damned her. If I had known, I would have said that Harmon was still in the

119

boathouse when I went inside, but Mimi and I thought we had nothing to hide."

I tightened my grip. "I know that Mimi didn't do it, Eric. I don't think Peter is convinced either, but the sheriff does have the authority to order an arrest."

The ripples started again. I pulled him away from the ears of the law, and once we were at a safe distance, added, "Listen, Eric, we know that Mimi is innocent. That means that someone else is guilty, and all we have to do is figure out who it is."

"Is that all?" Eric said woodenly.

He was clearly useless as a nominee for my Baker Street Irregulars, or even a bungling Watson. I gave him a brief lecture about self-control and efficiency in the face of disaster, then sent him away to worry about dinner. Peter caught me before I could perfect a scheme to incriminate Mrs. Robison-Dewitt by planting some vile bit of evidence on her person.

"Technically, Mimi is not under arrest yet," he told me as we started toward the porch. "Sheriff Lafleur wants to take her in for an official statement and further questioning, but he admits that the case is basically weak. No weapon so far, and a motive based on conflicting stories."

"Well, Eric's on the edge of a collapse. I hope Sheriff Lafleur—are you sure about that name?"

"Arlo Lafleur," Peter said gravely. "I checked his identification card."

"I hope he knows what he's doing," I said tartly. "What about this other investigation that you claim brought you here? If there is a perfectly legitimate felon—"

"It had nothing to do with Harmon Crundall. Those people involved in the—ah—other matter had no reason to murder Harmon. If they were going to kill someone, I imagine it would be me. And I'm still here."

"Then you won't tell me anything about it?" I said in a wounded voice. We both knew what it meant; I can be transparent, or at least translucent, when I take the trouble to do so.

He took my elbow to steer me away from the porch. When we were in the garden, he said, "I will tell you the essential details, but only so that I won't have you prowling around with some crazy scheme. However, I want your solemn promise—"

"Cross my heart." I swallowed a gloat.

He did not look terribly impressed by my avowed sincerity. After a moment of indecision, he relented and said, "We have seen a significant increase of drugs on the Farber campus in the last year. Not the so-called recreational drugs, but a colorful selection of amphetamines and barbiturates that are most popular around the end of the semester. Although we know where they're coming from, we haven't identified the campus distributor."

"The source being our favorite pharmaceutical salesman, Nickie Merrick," I said with a shrug. Too bad; I'd liked Nickie, and he was far better at playing detective than Peter. The oiled hair was an inspired touch. "Then he's passing the drugs to a student?"

"So we assume. However, he travels a great deal, and is only in Farberville on the weekends. He has been watched for months; his only contact remotely related to the campus is the theater. Other than that, he stays home. He does not bar-hop, stroll around campus with a briefcase, or inadvertently leave packages on park benches. No contact with anyone in Farberville except grocery clerks and gas station attendants."

"And the theater members who are also Farber students, such as Suzetta and Bruce?" I prompted.

"Those two, Eric Vanderhan, who teaches one class, and the three boys who were supposed to be Lieutenant Merrick's squad from Scotland Yard."

"Forget Eric. He is not a drug pusher. What do you know about the boys? They could very well be the ones you're after. They all have pasty complexions; maybe they've been in prison."

Peter tactfully overlooked my emotional outburst. "They joined the theater within the last few months, and the drugs have been inundating the campus since the fall." He narrowed his eyes at me. "It has nothing to do with Harmon's death."

"But he might have found out that his precious theater was being used to cover drug transactions. If he threatened to expose Nickie, then—"

"Harmon didn't have any idea about the drugs; Bella was quite sure about that point. She said that his behavior was perfectly normal—no worries, no secretive conversations. He was not a subtle man, and she swears she would have been able to tell if he were concerned about something that might harm the theater."

"What are you going to do about Nickie Merrick?" I said to change the subject. A conversation with Bella was called for, but I saw no need to discuss it with Peter.

"I have enough evidence to arrest him, but I want to take his campus contact at the same time. Merrick is still under observation. If he tries to make a deal, we'll be nearby. But I don't want him to sense anything that might deter him from his business, so forget this conversation—now."

"Of course." I told Peter that I wanted to check on Bella, in case she might be in the mood for a tray from the dining room or a bit of company. He raised an eyebrow, but finally left to return to the Mimosa Inn.

At the bungalow, I tapped on the door. Bella appeared from the bedroom, looking a good deal pinker.

"Claire, how nice of you to come by to check on me," she said through the screen. "I'm feeling better now, and I really would prefer to be alone to think about what has happened."

Her words caught me by surprise. I considered several options, including brute force, but finally said something inane and went back through the garden. As a detective, I was not a noticeable success. It was time for another suspect. Minutes later, another suspect landed in my arms in a metaphorical sprawl.

"Claire, I've been looking for you," Nickie Merrick called as I came out of the garden. He lowered his voice to a piercing stage whisper. "Do you think we might have a word in private?"

"By all means," I said with a gracious nod. The lawn was thickly populated, as was the porch and probably the drawing room. I was not about to invite a drug pusher into my bedroom for an intimate chat. "How about the boat-house?"

"Where Harmon was murdered? I don't think it's—"

"The body only stayed there a few hours," I said firmly, "and no one will disturb us. I didn't think Scotland Yard's finest would prove squeamish."

Looking less than delighted, Nickie opened the door for me and we went inside. Inches past the threshold, I let out an explosive sneeze. The shadowy recesses fluttered for an uneasy moment before subsiding into watchfulness.

"There must be some sort of mold in here," I said, wiping my eyes and blotting the end of my nose. "This is the only place that sets off this distasteful reaction."

"You're probably right, Claire. If the sneezing begins to interfere too much, let me know. I've got some samples of an antihistamine in my car. It's a new product and it's been quite effective with allergy sufferers. Very popular in the spring." He moved across the room to stare at the empty slip, still disturbed by my inspired choice of conference rooms. "So poor Harmon started his last boat ride here . . ."

"Did you hear that Mimi's been taken in for further questioning?" I sneezed emphatically to convey my disapproval.

"Bruce told me a few minutes ago. She seemed like such a nice girl; it's a damn shame. But I suppose Harmon must have gotten carried away with his role and made a pass at her, and she was forced to defend herself with a paddle. If only she hadn't tried to cover it up, she might have been able to claim self-defense."

"Mimi did not"—*sneeze!*—"murder Harmon!"

"Maybe not," he said, squatting to peer at a spider that had decided to relocate after what must have seemed a hurricane jolted his web. "Anyway, I hope the sheriff can get this over with before Monday morning. I have accounts to service and standing appointments that I can't afford to break. Some doctors are impossible to see without—"

"What did you want to discuss, Nickie?" I asked. Despite the casualness of his tone, I could tell that he was as nervous as Eric had been earlier. Very interesting. *Sneeze!*

"You appear to be on friendly terms with the cop from Faberville. I was wondering if he had said anything about me."

"Such as?"

"For one thing, was he satisfied with my statement? I wasn't completely candid. In fact, I kept certain things back in order to protect an innocent party."

"I have no idea whether Lieutenant Rosen was or was not satisfied with your statement, Nickie. It's not particularly wise to keep things from an officer investigating a homicide, though. That I learned from personal experience. If this person that you think you're protecting comes out with a different story, you're apt to find yourself in the cell adjoining Mimi's."

"Tell me what you think, then. I did leave the drawing room during the movie last night, but only for a minute or two. I did not go anywhere near the boathouse, not did I see anyone while I was outside."

"It sounds pretty frail," I said with a sympathetic smile that ended with a particularly loud sneeze. "If you didn't see or hear anything, then why should you refuse to admit that you slipped out? Was it not in your script?"

"No, I was never supposed to be a suspect, so I had nothing to do until this morning when I glowered at everyone over coffee." He stood up and straightened his tie with trembling hands. "I went outside to meet someone—but the person never came. It would have sounded bad, so I told Rosen that I didn't leave the room during the movie."

"Who never came?"

I knew it was his campus contact, but he didn't know that I knew. I held my breath and assumed a look of mild curiosity, although a trio of sneezes rather destroyed the effect. My bedroom would have been safer; I was in danger of jarring my nose out of position—permanently.

"It doesn't matter, Claire. The point is that I was outside for a few minutes, and I'm afraid it might be misconstrued if Rosen finds out about it later."

He was lying. He was afraid that Peter might have followed him, which was likely. However, and to my chagrin, I had no idea what Peter thought about Nickie's statement. I repeated the latter sentiment to Nickie and suggested that he confess to the sin of omission.

It was growing dark outside, and I could barely see Nickie's slow shake of his head. "Maybe later," he said as he opened the door for me. I sneezed a farewell to the spider, and went across the now deserted lawn to the inn.

Dinner was being served to a solemn group of guests, none of whom even glanced up when I entered the room. Caron was not there, nor was Peter. I heard Eric's voice in the kitchen; at last he was handling the mundane duties of innkeeper.

Nickie found two chairs in a corner table, and I allowed him to seat me. The gloomy miasma was impossible to resist; we ordered, ate, and exited to the drawing room as quickly as possible.

"At this point we were scheduled to unravel the mystery

and toast the winner with champagne," Nickie said in a wry voice. "This group would be livelier on a sewage disposal tour."

"Do you know who the mock murderer was to be?"

Nickie tugged on his moustache, his eyes on the closed office door. "Harmon wouldn't tell me. He thought I might give something away by an inadvertent inflection or beaded stare. Some of the others might know, Claire. Ask one of them."

Mimi was not available, and Eric was too distraught to handle more than one thing at a time. Nickie didn't know and Bella wasn't talking. My most likely stoolies were Suzetta and Bruce, but neither of them was in sight.

Suzetta had not been visible since the agonizing session in the dining room just after the murder was announced. It could be suspicious, I decided. It struck me that Peter had completely forgotten about her midnight prowl the night before, when he and I had bumped nose-to-pajama in the dark. She hadn't been dressed in rowing clothes, but one cannot be sure what constitutes appropriate attire for transporting one's murder victim.

I gave Nickie a vague wave and went to the register to find out Suzetta's room number. Then, a study in nonchalance, I glided upstairs for a girlish chat with the secretary/private eye/student who had a propensity for prowls.

All very good, but no one answered my discreet tap. I gave up and went along the corridor to my room, where I found my daughter still glued to the telephone. Her last call, I told myself coldly, as I remembered her treachery. She took in my expression, whispered a panicky farewell, and replaced the receiver.

"Did you find the cove on the far side of the lake?" she asked, shrinking into the bedspread. As well she should.

"Yes, and I found a cop waiting for me when I arrived. It seems he heard a bit of gossip on the road."

"Then you didn't have to walk back. Good, I was worried that you might get caught in the dark."

"You were worried about me? I thought your only concerns were the proximity of fish and your income." I stopped in front of the mirror. A twig clung to the top of my head like a tiny flagpole sans flag. My skin was crisscrossed by red scratches, my chin smudged with dust. Not an image that appealed. But Peter hadn't been deterred by my untidy appearance. . . . I put that disturbing memory aside and turned to glare at Caron.

"I was worried," she repeated. Her lip inched forward, her eyebrows toward each other. "You always think the worst about me, Mother. I happen to be a very sensitive person—you can ask any of the kids at school."

"I wouldn't dream of it. While we're on that subject, am I correct in assuming that Inez is well informed of the latest developments in the case?"

The lip ebbed, and gradually curled at the corners. "Inez agrees that I might be in danger. I swore that I would stay by the telephone in case someone tried to do something to me."

"A veritable umbilical cord of safety," I said, returning to the mirror to see if I might be worthy of salvage. "What is Inez going to do if the receiver is banged down in mid-scream? Call the operator to report a homicide, or call information to ask the identity of the strangler?"

"At least Inez is worried about me," Caron sniffled.

"A mere child, who has no knowledge of what has happened? You need to realign your pose, dear. In the meantime, you are not—repeat—not to speak to Peter Rosen unless he asks you a direct question. Your answer may range anywhere from 'yes' to 'no,' or perhaps a giddy 'I don't know.' If you do otherwise, you may plan to spend the next five years in your room, where you will subsist on bread, water, and broiled fish."

Caron plopped a pillow over her face. After a despairing

glance in the mirror, I decided to see if Suzetta might have
returned to her room. She had not. I tried the knob and
found that it turned easily. No one was in the corridor, and
half a second later neither was I.

Suzetta's bedroom was furnished the same as my own,
with an antique bed and the obligatory ceramic pitcher in a
bowl. The top of the dresser, however, was lost under an
array of bottles, tubes, brushes, and other paraphernalia
beyond my limited experience. I felt some satisfaction in
the knowledge that her beauty was not a simple task; my
semiannual Avon lady would have a coronary at the
potential income.

Humming under my breath, I studied the room for a clue,
although I wasn't at all confident that I would recognize one
if it crawled up my neck to kiss me on the ear. Beyond the
clutter on the dresser, the room was surprisingly neat.
Suzetta looked the type to drape clothes on the chair and
dangle nylon stockings from the shower rod, but the only
signs of occupancy in the bathroom were a blue toothbrush
beside a tube of toothpaste rolled neatly at the bottom, and
the wisp of a bikini hanging from a towel rack.

I opened the closet door, expecting chaos. Instead, I
found a raincoat, a tightly furled umbrella, a row of dresses
arranged in order of ascending skirt length, several pairs of
shoes, and two empty suitcases. No canoe paddle with bits
of blood and hair. A sneeze of disappointment exploded
from my decidedly sore nose; I was liable to be asked to
guide a sleigh if the case wasn't solved soon. I closed the
door and leaned against it while I waited for inspiration.

If Suzetta had not gone outside in the middle of the night
to dispose of her corpse, then she had gone for another
purpose. Wonderful, Claire. I forced myself to recall the
scene in detail. There had been a rumble in the parking lot
shortly before Suzetta slipped out the back door. More
wonderful, but not helpful; Suzetta hadn't been the rumbler.
But it did mean that someone else was on the prowl at the
same time.

"Nickie!" I said aloud, charmed by the success of my mental gymnastics. Obviously, Suzetta was the student whose extracurricular activities were of interest to Peter. One of them had been obliged to silence Harmon. Suzetta had subsequently slipped outside to do the sculling, and Nickie had taken his car to meet her when she came out of the woods. It wasn't particularly gallant of him, but he could not be accused of chauvinism. Maybe he had no experience with small craft. Something like that. In any case, she had indeed gone outside to dispose of her corpse.

It was as good as any explanation for all the midnight activity. Bella was quite simply wrong. The illicit drug activity *was* the motive for Harmon's murder, and Mimi could be cleared before Eric slithered into total depression. Now all I needed was evidence to confirm the brilliant deduction. A tiny capsule would be adequate.

I dropped to my knees and began to crawl around the perimeter of the room, asking myself where I would be if I were an amphetamine. After five fruitless minutes, I determined that I would not be on the floor. I then confirmed that I would not be in the bathroom or in a plastic vial amidst the perfume bottles, nor in the suitcases in the closet. The dresser drawers remained.

I was digging through a pile of brightly colored scarves when the bedroom door opened behind me. I sat back on my heels and gazed into Suzetta's surprised—and displeased—eyes.

"I came by to ask you something," I said brightly, "but you weren't here."

Suzetta continued to stare down at me, her arms crossed and her lips squeezed into a white line. The brainless giggles were more than absent; they were a contradiction that now seemed incredible. I would have welcomed a hint of a simper or a flutter of the patently false eyelashes. The woman was far too pissed to oblige.

I tried again. "I did so admire the scarves that you wore

to the costume party, Suzetta. You must tell me where you bought them." When she failed to lapse into the familiar routine, I leaned forward and ran my fingers through the silk rainbow.

We both saw the glint of metal, a cold, bluish-gray glint totally unsuitable for jewelry. It was, however, perfect for a gun. I jammed a red scarf over it and scrambled to my feet.

"Thanks for letting me look at your scarves. I'll see you at breakfast," I said, moving around her toward the door.

Unfortunately, Suzetta arrived at the door first. Holding the knob with white knuckles, she said, "I don't want you to rush off like this, Claire. I haven't told you where to find the scarves, and I can see how much you admire them. Why don't you sit over there?"

It was not an invitation. Reminding myself that we were equidistant from the lethal contents of the drawer, I did as told. "Where did you get the scarves, Suzetta?"

"From a discount house, although I doubt that you'll race out to buy them anytime soon." She sat down on the bed to study me with a detached coldness. "What were you searching for?"

Oh, dear. It did not seem wise to tell her that I was searching for her stash of illegal substances, but the scarf story did sound weak. Then again, I wasn't going to learn anything if I scampered out of the room like a puppy that had piddled on the rug. As long as the gun—why did she of all people have a gun?—remained in the drawer, I was safe. Surely.

I leaned back and crossed my legs. If I'd had my knitting bag, I might have whipped out a half-finished bootie à la Miss Marple and clicked away. "I saw you sneak out of the inn last night after everyone was supposedly tucked in bed."

"And . . . ?" she drawled, not noticeably distressed.

"I thought it was suspicious."

"That hardly explains why you decided to search my room."

A valid point. I uncrossed my legs and put away the mental bootie. "I was looking for evidence."

"Evidence of what?"

It was not going well. Suzetta was not in tears, eager to confess her evil business with a drug dealer. She wasn't admitting to a tryst, or looking particularly guilty, for that matter. To my annoyance, she seemed to be increasingly relaxed. I was going to be forced to go for the jugular—if I wanted a confession.

"Evidence of what?" she repeated in the maddening drawl.

"Evidence of your illegal drug trafficking!"

Her mouth fell open, and her eyelashes did a second's worth of the old flutter. "My illegal drug trafficking? You must be kidding!"

"I am not kidding. Look, Suzetta, Lieutenant Rosen already knows that you're the link between Nickie Merrick and the students at Farber College. There's no point in trying to avoid any reprisal, but I think the Lieutenant might be willing to negotiate. I'm sure the whole scheme was Nickie's idea, and . . ."

Suzetta had managed to close her mouth and restrain the flutters. In the midst of what I felt to be the most inspirational moment of my sermon, she had also managed to reach the dresser. I ran out of kindly advice when the gun was pointed at my face. The round hole at the end of the barrel was larger than one might have suspected, and very black.

"Get up," she said. "We're going for a little walk."

"You wouldn't dare shoot me," I countered calmly. This is not to say that I was feeling especially calm, and I hoped she couldn't hear my heart rotating as if it were impaled on a spit.

Suzetta flicked the gun at the door before centering it

once again on my nose. "Get up, Claire. You might discover that you have no idea what I will do."

Indeed. I walked to the door. After draping a sweater over the gun, she jabbed it into my side and said, "Don't do anything heroic. We're going to walk downstairs and through the back door to the stable to continue this absurd conversation. If you make any signs or try to escape, you'll find your internal organs have become external."

"What a tacky thing to say."

"But true . . ."

I marched out the door, refusing to acknowledge the painful little jabs to my spine. As I passed my bedroom door, I willed Caron to open it so that I could at least try to communicate the situation. I could have wished for a pig in a tutu to pirouette past me—and had better odds.

A door did open as we reached the top of the staircase, but it was not my ideal choice of a rescuer. Mrs. Robison-Dewitt came out of her room, snorted as she saw me, and nodded regally to Suzetta. Had she known the danger I was in, no doubt she would have applauded. In oblivious splendor she continued down the corridor, knocked on a door, and was admitted without further ado.

I glanced back at Suzetta. "Mrs. Robison-Dewitt will remember seeing us together. You'll never get away with this, so you might as well put down the gun and—" I broke off to grasp at the sudden jolt to my ribcage. "I was trying to help."

"You've already helped too much," Suzetta said coldly.

We went downstairs and turned toward the back door. The door to the office opened, and Peter stepped into my path. "Where are you two going?"

"Out for a walk," I croaked. I received a jab as a reward.

Ignoring my rather strained expression, Peter smiled benignly. "What a nice idea. Well, I'll see you later, girls. Enjoy your little walk."

I doubted that I would enjoy the little walk for long.

Since it was hopeless in any case, I closed my eyes, took a breath, and screeched, "Arrest her, Peter! She has a gun on me!"

Contrary to all expectations, a bullet did not rip through my back to modify my organs and carry me into the great unknown. The pressure was released, and suddenly I heard a most startling sound: laughter, coming from behind me. Gleeful, lilting laughter, as if the clowns had just catapulted their cream pies.

I whirled around. Suzetta was making helpless noises as tears rolled down her cheeks. The gun swung about in an aimless pattern, its owner too convulsed to concern herself with the display of incriminating evidence.

"What is going on?" I demanded.

"She was searching my room," Suzetta sputtered. "I'm sorry, but I just couldn't help myself." She lapsed into laughter again, although she did lower the gun before Aunt Beatrice's chandelier was decimated.

"What is going on?" I repeated, ready to choke off the laughter with my bare hands.

Peter produced another benign smile. "I believe you're under arrest, Claire."

TEN

It was preferable to being shot, but only by a narrow margin. I waited until Suzetta choked out a final laugh, then raised my eyebrows and politely said, "Would someone care to explain?"

"Why don't we go in here?" Peter said, holding open the office door. "It's—ah, complicated."

We went in the office and found chairs. Peter was clearly loving every minute of it, and Suzetta let out an occasional chuckle. I, on the other hand, was neither delighted nor warmed by the merriment I had unwittingly afforded them.

"Exactly how complicated is it?" I said when we were as cozy as a trio of cowboys around a campfire. It came out rather nicely, considering the proximity of the coyotes and/or rattlesnakes.

"Miss Price works for me," he said. He smiled at the blonde, who dimpled and produced a flattering blush. When I blush, I am slightly less attractive than a withered geranium, and the only dimple I possess is not conveniently situated for public admiration.

"That's correct, I've been under cover on the drug

operation for over eight months. Lieutenant Rosen is my boss." And her idol; we could all hear the unspoken words.

"How fascinating, for both of you!" I said. "First, you were a retarded secretary, who turned into a private eye, who turned into a student, who turned into an undercover cop. How utterly, utterly fascinating. However, this is not the land of Oz, and I don't believe in Munchkins or tap-dancing scarecrows." I stood up and stomped toward the door.

"Claire, please come back and sit down," Peter said. Sincerity oozed from his voice.

I forced myself to comply. Not out of any desire to cooperate, of course, but from a need to pump as much information out of the two baboons as possible. If Suzetta didn't kill Harmon, then I needed a new direction. And for once, I could play the aggrieved victim.

"Well?" I said in a sour voice.

"Let Suzetta tell me what happened first," he said with another dollop of sincerity.

Suzetta briskly reported finding me in her room and repeated verbatim the subsequent conversation, although she embellished my bewilderment and my final ill-judged conclusion. She managed to maintain a professional tone, but it was obvious that she had found the whole scene much more entertaining than her last birthday party.

When she was done, Peter looked at me. "I thought you promised to stay out of the investigation, Claire."

Back on the carpet in front of the principal, who was growing weary of reprimanding me. It was mutual. I shrugged and said, "I was trying to clear Mimi before Eric cracked up. You know that she didn't bash Harmon over the head."

Suzetta laughed. "Is she under cover, too, Lieutenant Rosen? I thought I knew everyone in the CID."

"Claire's beyond 'undercover.' She's Farbervile's most—"

"Sorry to interrupt," I interrupted, my blood back to a simmer. "Shall we discuss something more pertinent—such as Harmon's murder or even the identity of Nickie's campus pusher? If you weren't sneaking out last night to take a shipment of drugs from Nickie or to transport Harmon, then what were you doing?" I asked Suzetta.

Peter nodded to her. She said, "I went to search Bruce Wheeler's room for evidence of drugs."

"Where was Bruce at the time?"

"Bruce drove Harmon's car down the road and parked it. Harmon was supposed to sneak away from the boathouse to meet him and then drive home. He was worried that he might be seen if he went to the stable to get his car, when the script called for him to be already dead." Suzetta held up a finger to cut off my question. "No, I did not find any evidence that linked Bruce to Nickie. It seems as though I'd better try to search Eric's bedroom."

I muttered a perfunctory protest. Suzetta was no longer available to fill in any roles in my hypothesized plot. I did not want to consider the possibility that Mimi was a murderer and Eric a drug dealer, although it was looking more likely every minute. Sighing, I looked at Peter.

"Bruce did what he was supposed to do?"

"He left the car about a half mile down the road, and waited almost an hour for Harmon to appear. Harmon couldn't make it, for known reasons. Eventually, Bruce gave up and went back to his room."

"What happened to Harmon's car?"

"I was examining it this morning when the Audubon group spilled out of the woods in a twitter. Later, it was examined again, then brought back to the stable. Mrs. Crundall now has the keys."

"I don't suppose the trunk was filled with drugs?" Grasping at straws in a hurricane, I admit.

Peter dismissed Suzetta, who gave me a wink as she strolled out of the door. I did not reciprocate. Across the desk, Peter grimaced and said, "The trunk was empty, Claire. I don't want to arrest Eric on a drug charge, and I would prefer to see him and his wife cleared of any suspicion. But my job is harder when I have to spend a certain amount of my time rescuing you from a variety of sticky situations."

Familiar and tedious. I retreated to the offensive position that had worked earlier. "Why did you allow that woman to terrorize me with a gun, and pretend she was going to blow my head off and bury me in a pile of manure in the stable"?

"Her reactions were spontaneous. I did not instruct her to pull a gun on you, should she find you in her room," he said, all teeth and honey. "I did warn her that you might decide to visit, however."

"Good for you; maybe you can retire from the police department and earn a living as a gypsy fortune-teller."

"Maybe I ought to. It might be easier than putting up with your attempts to emulate Miss Marple. Is there anything else you've discovered in your amateur, unauthorized, harebrained investigation?"

I grudgingly repeated my conversation with Nickie. "He must have gone outside to meet his contact," I concluded, "although the person in question stood him up. It was undoubtedly Mrs. Robison-Dewitt; she has the aura of a felon."

"But not of a student." Peter stood up and escorted me to the door. "Claire, please let me handle this. If you insist on continuing, I may suggest to Suzetta that she file burglary charges."

"I thought the Gestapo was disbanded at the end of World War II."

"That's the current theory," he murmured. The door closed firmly in my face.

Mentally composing prickly comments about eavesdroppers and supercilious cops, I went into the drawing room and sat down to plan the next siege. I dismissed the drug

mess for the moment and turned my thoughts to the murder.
The door to the porch had been a revolving door between
ten o'clock and midnight. Suzetta, Mimi, Eric, and Bruce
had all left on various scripted missions. Nickie had gone to
meet a no-show, who might have been any of the mentioned
or someone else. Harmon was in the boathouse, playing out
his wonderful scenario. Bella was in her bungalow, drinking
tea and brandy. I was in the parlor, sleeping through the
movie. All I needed was a blackbird to snip off my nose, if
the sneezes didn't do it first.

I decided I ought to drop a tactful word of warning to
Eric. I found him in the kitchen, perched on the same stool
that Mimi had occupied earlier. He was pale, too tired to do
more than twitch his mouth in greeting as I joined him.

"Mimi called from the sheriff's office," he said. "She
told me that she would probably be there all night and to call
a lawyer in the morning. What can I do, Claire? She
didn't—she didn't—kill Harmon. Why would she have
done that?"

"Everyone knows about the option, Eric. It gives both of
you one of the more mundane motives in homicide cases:
self-preservation."

"But Harmon wasn't going to exercise the option," Eric
said. He sagged so violently, I worried he would topple off
the stool. "I told him that. I mean, I told the sheriff that.
Oh, hell, I don't know what I told anybody. . . . " His
voice died in a plaintive whisper.

"If you and Mimi want to keep the Mimosa Inn, you're
going to have to pull yourself together," I said sternly, not
at all sure that I could lift him off the floor if he continued in
this vein. "Bella told Peter that Harmon intended to use the
optioned property for a subdivision to be called Harmony
Hills. That doesn't sound as though he was planning to let it
expire."

"She's lying," he mumbled.

"Why would she lie about it? And while we're on the

subject, where is this infamous option? Mimi said that it was to be burned and the ashes used as clues. Suzetta found a blank option and burned that without giving it much thought. So where is it now?"

"I don't know, Claire, and I don't care. I need to get Mimi out of that jail before she breaks down. She's more delicate than she appears to outsiders. She's like a mimosa leaf; if you touch one, it shrinks and folds up."

Eric may have enjoyed the imagery, but I suspected Mimi was a good bit sturdier than the analogy implied. Eric, on the other hand, bore no resemblance to the quick-witted mathematician I had known. We needed to get Mimi back for his sake, not hers.

I gave him a rallying poke and said, "Tell me exactly what you said in your statement, and anything else you may have overlooked."

"I started the movie at about ten o'clock. Before that, I went upstairs and overheard Mimi talking to Harmon, which is when the mud was supposed to fall off my shoe in the hall, except that I forgot to pick it up when I was outside earlier. So I waited until ten-thirty, when I went to the boathouse. Well, I was a minute late because of a question, and I had to go across the croquet court, and that reminded me about the mud, so I picked up a piece to leave later and—"

"Never mind," I said. How the man ever learned to count, much less to make forays into calculus and other murky fields, was hard to imagine. Sequencing was not a visible strength. "Tell me what you saw at the boathouse— or didn't see."

He stared into space. "As I came out on the porch, I saw Mimi leave. I gave her time to cut across the yard to the back door, then went to the boathouse and called to Harmon. He didn't answer, and it was too dark to see anything. For a minute or two, I thought he was fooling around. But he wasn't there, Claire."

"But Mimi said he was and that she talked to him," I said patiently. "Did he fly out a window?"

"There aren't any windows. The sheriff says that Mimi bashed Harmon on the head and hid his body in the rowboat. I didn't look in the rowboat; it was too dark and I couldn't have seen anything, anyway."

"So what did you do then?"

"Well, I decided that he had changed the plans without telling me. He could have warned Mimi that he wasn't going to be there, but that she was supposed to pretend that he was. I slipped back to the movie projector with plenty of time for the reel change."

"But Mimi swears that he was there when she left—and that he was alive. If we accept that, we'll have to come up with an explanation for Harmon's vanishing act. Are you positive no one went in the boathouse between the time Mimi left and you arrived?"

"I could see the door the entire time, Claire. It was dark, but there was enough moonlight and overflow from the upstairs windows." Eric made a strangled noise and began to tremble.

I quickly opted for a new topic. "After Mimi went in the back door, what did she do?"

"She met Suzetta in our bedroom to confirm that the option was burned, then they came back in time for the lights to go on at the end of the movie. After that, we locked up and went to bed."

What a muddle, I sighed to myself. I did not want Eric to sense my discouragement, so I managed a jolly smile. "Don't worry; we'll figure it out. Up until Harmon disappeared, everyone was acting according to his or her script, right? Did anyone do anything that seemed inappropriate?"

"I don't know, Claire; Harmon had the script. Do you think I ought to go to the sheriff's office and tell them that I lied, that Harmon was there when I arrived? I could say that he said something about the option, so I—"

"No, Eric," I said hastily, "you're likely to make things worse. The sheriff has doubts about the motive; for God's sake, don't drop by to confirm it. I need to get my hands on Harmon's master script. Mimi thought it was in the office, but Peter said he searched for it. Can you think of any place else it might be?"

"Harmon's room, maybe."

"Why don't you go upstairs and search for it, then? We need to compare everyone's actions with the script to see if anyone improvised something radically different. Look for the option while you're there. Go!" I said, shooing him out of the kitchen with a maternal eye and an encouraging look.

Eric did as ordered. I waited until I heard a quiet click from the top of the stairs, then climbed on the stool. Lofty, but not helpful. My first realization was that I did not care for heights, even of the three-foot sort. The second was that the staff had not done a very good job on the countertops. The third was that I was confused by the whole mess and wanted to go home to my bookstore, where things fit into polite categories. Here, I could not isolate fiction from nonfiction.

Begin at the beginning, I lectured myself. I did well until I arrived at the log in the cove. I could not stir up any regret; on the contrary, more primitive feelings rose like sparks from an open fire, heat and all. Unlike the mimosa leaf, I hadn't folded on contact. Not in the least. After some introspection, I concluded that no action was required on the matter, or was advisable.

I moved on to the last few hours of the melodrama. Bella's name had popped up from several different sources. Bella had sworn that Harmon knew nothing of the drug transactions happening backstage at the Faberville Community Theater; Bella had sworn that Harmon was indeed prepared to exercise the option. Bella had been talkative to everyone except Miss Claire Marple.

I wrote her name in the soapy film on the countertop. She had made as many transformations as Suzetta: dowdy mouse, hysterical wife, decisive woman, grieving widow, self-imposed exile. And motor-mouth extraordinaire. Surely, I deserved a few words.

It was too late for a proper neighborly call, but I hadn't come up with another excuse as I knocked on the bungalow door. "Bella? It's Claire. I thought you might be in the mood for a little company."

She came out of the bedroom, wearing her coat over jeans and a sweater. "Claire," she murmured, "how kind of you."

"Are you going out?" At ten o'clock?"

"No, dear, I just returned from a walk in the rose garden. I was afraid the lime might have burned the roses' roots, so I went to see if they were drooping." She shrugged off her coat and gestured for me to come inside. "Would you like a cup of tea? It's my turn to play hostess."

"Yes, thank you, I would. This day has been one of the longest in my life, exceeded only by the day I went into labor with Caron and the day my husband was killed in a car wreck. I can imagine how you must feel."

"It has been trying. By now, the only thing Lieutenant Rosen doesn't know about me is my shoe size and my secret fondness for chocolate mint ice cream."

"I have a problem with almond fudge," I admitted. A familiar tickle crept down my nose. I rubbed frantically, first with a ladylike finger and then with my whole hand. As the tickle abated, I realized Bella was watching me with a perplexed expression.

"Is something wrong?" she asked.

"Allergies. Nickie said he had some samples that might help; I may have to beg for them." A lovely cue. "Did Peter tell you about the drug problem at Farber and the theater connection?"

She gave me a cup and saucer, then sat down across from

me. "He did, but I fail to see any relevance to Harmon's . . . death. If my husband had been suspicious, he would have confided in me. He was quite fond of Nickie." She paused, then added, "He was fond of Mimi, too. It's so difficult to believe she could have done such a dreadful thing."

"I don't believe it," I said flatly.

"The sheriff sat in on my statement, and he became quite agitated when I mentioned Harmony Hills. Apparently, Mimi and Eric lied about it when they gave their statements. I don't understand that, either. Harmon was quite determined to go through with the project; ironically, he wanted to invest the profits in a new theater building."

"At the expense of destroying the Mimosa Inn. Are you quite sure Mimi and Eric knew his plans?"

"Quite sure, dear. I'm sorry."

I did not like the way things were going. "Tell me about Harmon," I suggested. "All I saw was the role he played, which was distressingly adept. What was he really like?"

Bella went to the dinette to take a pack of cigarettes out of her purse. As I waited, the dreaded nose tickle caught me by surprise and I sneezed explosively.

"I'll get pills from Nickie," I vowed before Bella could offer sympathy or a tissue.

She gave me a doubtful smile, lit a cigarette, and sat down again. "Harmon was a kind man, who doted on the students at the theater as if they were his offspring. We had no children, you see, and he used them as replacements. He encouraged them to bring their problems to him, and often loaned them money or wrote glowing letters of recommendation."

"He had his theater troupe; you had your chemistry students."

"I still have my students, even if I no longer have Harmon. I'm looking forward to returning to my routine Monday morning—if your policeman allows us to leave."

"I have no idea what he intends to do," I said, displeased with her description. "Sheriff Lafleur may decide that the investigation is completed; in that case, Peter may agree and let us leave. Are you going to teach classes Monday morning? Shouldn't you take a leave of absence for a few weeks?"

"To sit home and mope? No, Claire, my students need me—and I need the diversion. Their eternal ineptness in chemistry lab will help to take my mind off things."

"Then it's probably best," I murmured. When Carlton was killed, I had stayed home and moped, and it had served no useful purpose. "What about the funeral?"

"On Wednesday at four o'clock. Perhaps I'll see you there, dear. For now, I'm still a bit tired, and I think I'll go to bed." She went across the room to hold open the door for me.

I tried a final shot. "What will happen to Harmony Hills now? Will you see the project through, or let the option expire?"

"Harmony Hills will be built as a tribute to my husband."

I opened my mouth to mention the missing option, but found I was about to speak to solid wood. Ah, well, I told myself as I walked along the path through the garden. The marble cupid was a pale ghost in the moonlight, forever optimistic, waiting.

"Do you realize that you may be gazing at 'cul-dee-saxes' in the near future?" I asked him sternly. In moments of confusion, I have been known to talk to inanimate objects. A symptom of schizophrenia, or so I've been warned. Thus far, nothing has answered.

Except for a drowsy deputy on the porch, no one was about. A line of light shone from under the office door, but I went upstairs without allowing myself to toy with the idea of a chat with "my policeman," who had done nothing constructive about Mimi's arrest, the unidentified drug pusher, or my ambivalent attitude toward him.

"Phooey!" I muttered under my breath as I went into the room I shared with my daughter the squealer.

Caron was sitting in the middle of the bed, a book held not more than two inches from her nose. It was upside down, which was a rather unmissable clue to her former activity.

"Did Inez have any pertinent comments about postpubescent child abuse?" I asked as I undressed and pulled on a night shirt.

"I happen to have been reading." She noticed that the book was somewhat illegible from its present perspective, and put it down. "Not really, but she does know some of the people—or *of* them, anyway."

"How clever of her. She knows you, me, and Peter—not a bad batting average. This impresses you?" I sat down at the dressing table and began to dab calamine lotion on each red bump and welt. I estimated there were four thousand; I might still be dabbing at sunrise.

"And someone else." Caron picked up the book and made a pretense of fascination with the written word, now upright.

I dabbed diligently for a long moment. When I could no longer restrain myself from taking the proffered carrot, I said, "And who might that be?"

She flipped to the next page, read it with great concentration, dogeared the corner, and carefully placed the book on the floor beside the bed. I was going to suffer for all the indignities of the last two days, fish threats and all. In the interim I dabbed twenty-nine bumps. After Caron was satisfied with her petty revenge, she lay back on the bed, crossed her arms over her chest, sighed grandly, and said, "The guy's wife."

"The guy's wife? That narrows it down to the female half of those present, excepting you. Could you be more precise?" I forced myself to dab a nasty red bump just below my earlobe. It could pass for a ruby earring if it continued to swell at the present rate.

"Did you ever see the creepy old movie about vampires?"

"I do not see the relevance of my cinema attendance record. If you intend to drag this out until September, let me know now. Otherwise, please get on with it."

"Well . . . Inez's sister Julianna goes to Farber High School, and she has junior chemistry with Mrs. Crundall."

"The earth trembles under my feet. Would you mind putting some lotion on my back? I can't reach all the mosquito bites, and I'm afraid they'll keep me awake tonight."

"Don't you want to know what Julianna thinks of Mrs. Crundall?" Caron growled, outraged by my lack of interest in adolescent gossip. "It could be vital, Mother."

I tossed the tube of lotion at her. "I am still stunned by the knowledge that Inez has a sister. The idea of an older version of Inez gives me goose bumps."

"Those are mosquito bites," Caron said coldly. "Julianna is terribly perceptive, and she told Inez all sorts of things about Mrs. Crundall. But if you don't care"—pout, pout, pout—"we'll drop the subject."

"I apologize," I said, watching her in the mirror. The pouts might keep me awake long after the itches subsided. "What did Juliette tell Inez?"

"Julianna!"

"What did Julianna tell Inez that Inez found worthy of repeating to you?" I said humbly.

"For one thing, the kids call Mrs. Crundall 'Bella Lugosi' because she's so awful. Just like the actor that played Count Dracula in the movies."

"High-school teachers often earn unflattering nicknames. I had an English teacher once—"

"She is the very worst teacher at the high school. The

kids in her class have hours of homework every single night, and in class she bawls them out all the time."

"Ghastly stuff. Are you sure Julianna isn't exaggerating because she doesn't understand the nature of molecules?" I said, trying to be reasonable without risking another bout of pouts.

"Julianna is a straight-A student," Caron sniffed. "And she says that all the kids hate Bella Lugosi-Crundall. After all, she's a cheerleader."

"Mrs. Crundall?"

"Julianna, Mother. Mrs. Crundall is a horrid teacher and a mean person—and everybody hates her."

"That's strange," I said, mostly to myself. "Bella implied that she felt like a surrogate mother to her students."

"Snow White's stepmother believed the same thing," Caron said. She looked at the telephone, stared at me, and with reluctance picked up her book. "I think the woman is capable of anything, including murder!" she announced before diving into her book.

From the mouths of babes, I told myself as I applied a final blob of calamine. I now resembled a clown who had been caught in a thundershower, but I wasn't going anywhere. Ignoring Caron's huffs, I found my notebook and flipped through the pages.

There were several heavily underlined observations that no longer had significance. Suzetta had been on duty when she had prowled out the back door. I drew a line through it. Bruce had produced the rumble in order to take Harmon's car to the assigned meeting place. I drew another line. For exercise I drew an irritable slash through every terse reference to Suzetta. Nickie had admitted that he had left the drawing room during the movie, but he wouldn't have been so candid if he had murdered Harmon. Slash on Nickie. No drugs in Bruce's room—slash. Mimi and Eric

deserved a slash as an act of faith, so I marked them off the
list.

One name remained.

A faint snore drifted from the bed. I crept around the
room until I was dressed in jeans and a sweater. Then,
feeling as silly as usual in such circumstances, I quietly
closed the door behind me and tiptoed down the stairs.

ELEVEN

It was nearly midnight by this time. A small lamp on the desk provided enough light for me to wind a path through Aunt Beatrice's furniture to the front door. I slipped out to the porch and eased the door closed.

I had company. Two figures sat on the swing, shoulders touching and heads an inch apart. The swing creaked softly, but the two figures could have passed for cardboard props.

"Who's there?" I squeaked.

"Bruce Wheeler."

"Oh, Bruce, you almost gave me a heart attack," I said as I went over to the swing. "Who's with you?"

"This is Alvin McGig. He's a busboy. We're both off duty now, and we weren't disturbing anyone until you came along."

"It's fine with me," I began defensively, "if you want to"—I realized that they were holding hands. Oh, dear— "swing on the porch, Bruce. I thought it seemed like a nice night for a stroll, myself. The moon is so—high, and the stars are, too."

"Enjoy yourself."

Alvin giggled, but broke off in a hiccup when Bruce glared at him. I waved a hand in farewell and managed a decorous pace until I reached the edge of the garden. As soon as I was concealed by shrubbery, I stumbled to the bench and sank down before my legs disgraced me in front of my marble friend.

Bruce's questionable story was now explained. My virile beach boy would have bleached his tan before admitting to his unconventional preference for the same gender. Naturally, he had not cared to discuss the goal of his late-night walks; Alvin McGig's company was a dubious reward. Grimacing, I pulled myself up. A whisper put me back on the bench.

"Claire?"

It was either a giant mosquito or Peter Rosen. To my regret, it proved to be the latter. He stepped from behind the cupid—my cupid—and joined me.

"Out for a breath of fresh air?" he teased as he sat down beside me. "I thought you preferred the canned, filtered, mechanically cooled variety?"

"I do. It seems I'm allergic to whatever they use around here. What are you doing, if I may be so bold?"

"Waiting for you. Were you heading for Bella's bungalow? Don't let me delay you further."

"Did you follow me to the bungalows yesterday, too?"

"Only in my dreams. It must have been some other white knight."

Oh, so silky. I sulked for a few minutes, while I considered the limitations imposed by his unexpected presence. On the one hand, I saw no reason to share the upcoming glory that would come with my brilliant solution. On the other, I saw no reason to be bashed on the head and rowed across the lake, face down in an inch of mucky water. Miss Marple sat by a cozy fire and chatted reminiscently about parlor maids and vicars; her attentive policeman then undertook the more dangerous tasks. Perhaps that's why she finished so many booties.

"I've been thinking," I announced reluctantly. I ran through the process by which I had eliminated all but one of the suspects. My voice paled when I described the scene on the porch, but recovered and ended in triumph.

"That sounds quite good," Peter said, "but we have no evidence that Bella was ever in the boathouse, much less that she murdered her husband. If you have no qualms about potential slander suits, you can race around making accusations. I can't—without proof."

"Bella was in the boathouse," I insisted.

"She didn't carve her initials in the door."

"No, but she brought the evidence with her back to the bungalow," I said, suddenly excited. "The only site that sets off my sneezes is the boathouse, because of a particular type of mold in there. Earlier, when I dropped by the bungalow, my nose started to tickle—and Bella's coat was next to me on the sofa."

"I'm not sure your nose will hold up in court." He leaned over to study the object under discussion. "You're covered with blotches, Claire. Are you developing some rare skin disorder?"

"That was not amusing. I can prove that Bella was in the boathouse, if I have to sneeze in front of the jury to do it. Now, all we need is motive and—"

"Claire, slow down. Even if she did visit the boathouse, she may have done so at any time in the last twenty-four hours. This afternoon, for instance, or yesterday before Harmon went out for the staged rendezvous with Mimi. Mimi swears that he was alive when she left; less than two minutes later he was gone—in the terminal sense. How did Bella manage to squeeze in between Mimi and Eric?"

"I don't know. I do know that she was in the boathouse, and it wasn't to watch the spider races. Besides that, the woman is a liar. She led me to believe that she was a doting mother hen to her dear students, but Caron's friend Inez says her nickname is Bella Lugosi. If Bella lied about that, maybe she lied about everything."

"High-school kids are not notoriously accurate in their character judgments. I had a biology teacher once—"

"Well, I'm going to ask her. Are you coming?" The last was tossed over my shoulder as I started toward the far side of the garden.

Looking less than thrilled at the invaluable opportunity, Peter accompanied me to the bungalow. The light was on, and behind the curtains a figure moved about the main room. A good omen, since I wasn't confident enough to pound on the door and demand an explanation—or a confession. A gentle knock sufficed.

"Claire . . . and Lieutenant Rosen, what a charming surprise," Bella said without enthusiasm. "Would you like to come in for tea or a quick nightcap?"

"Thank you," I said. I pulled Peter inside, aimed him at the sofa, and made a vague gesture in the direction of the stove. "Let me help you with the cups, Bella."

When we were settled, Bella turned shrewd eyes on us. "A bit late for a social call, isn't it? Was there something in particular that you had in mind?"

"Yes," I said before Peter could swallow his mouthful of tea, "I was curious about your visit to the boathouse."

"Are you, dear? I didn't realize that anyone knew about that." Bella sat back and rewarded me with a broad smile.

"The mold." I went to the closet and opened the door. Bella's coat politely precipitated the desired nasal explosion. I shot a smug smile at Peter, then sat down, wiped my eyes, and looked at my suspect. "Was Harmon surprised to see you, or had you mentioned the planned visit before hand?"

"I decided to drop by while he was awaiting Mimi. We had a few marital details to discuss, and I knew I wouldn't see him again until Sunday morning. He was supposed to go home for the day, you know, and return for brunch Sunday morning." She took a sip of tea. "Harmon did love a lavish brunch, especially the cheese grits and biscuits."

Peter opened his mouth. I elbowed him and quickly said, "Did you and Harmon have a nice visit?"

"He was quite alive when I left," Bella replied serenely. "Mimi can confirm that."

"What time was that?"

"She was scripted to arrive around ten-thirty, but you'll have to ask her if she was prompt. I don't wear a watch." She held up a wrist to show us the timelessness of it.

I found myself gaping at the still visible scratches. Beside me, Peter gulped down his tea and returned my earlier jab. While I was recovering, he said, "Where did those come from, Mrs. Crundall? From a walk around the lake in the dark, when the thorns are impossible to avoid?"

"Hardly, Lieutenant. Claire can tell you that I did some work in the garden. I cannot bear to see roses neglected so cruelly."

"She was digging there this morning," I admitted. After a moment of thought, I added, "Is that when your shoes picked up the mud? A clump of mud was found in Harmon's room. Everyone assumed that Eric had left it—according to his script. But he told me this evening that he had forgotten it . . . and it was an odd shade of gray. From the lime, I imagine."

She fumbled through her purse for her cigarettes. When she had lit one, she shrugged. "I did go to Harmon's room after I left the boathouse. I didn't notice the mud, and I forgot that the pseudo-detectives were going to crawl around with magnifying glasses." She inhaled deeply, then allowed the smoke to drift out in lazy, guiltless curlicues. "Harmon was alive when Mimi arrived, dear. You mustn't forget that."

A sticky problem. I looked at Peter. "Well?"

"Mimi insists that he was." He turned a choirboy smile

on Bella. "Did you find the option and carry it away before it could be burned?"

"Harmon was acting like a benevolent uncle instead of a business man," Bella said with the first trace of anger we had seen. "He swore that the option would go up in smoke—along with several hundred thousand dollars of potential profit. I saw no purpose in that, so I did go to his room to remove the option. He had several blank forms in his briefcase; I merely substituted for the vital one."

"Is it here now?" I asked.

"Yes, it is. I have an appointment with my lawyer Monday morning to see how best to proceed. He mentioned some sort of emergency order from a probate judge; the exact details escape me."

"You drove to Farberville earlier this evening," I said. "You told me that you had been walking in the garden."

"Did I? How peculiar of me to confuse the two activities."

"Very," I agreed. "So you intend to exercise the option yourself, even if the Mimosa Inn is ruined?"

"As quaint as the scenery may be, I would perfer to see it filled with ranch houses, and my bank account filled as well. Then, overcome with grief from my tragic and untimely loss, I'll submit my resignation and head for Europe on the next ocean liner. I think I'd enjoy an outside cabin, or even a suite."

"What about your precious flower garden?"

"I'll be able to afford a gardener, dear. I understand some of the botanical gardens in Holland are simply fabulous."

"And your students?"

She smiled again. "They can blow their precious heads off in chemistry lab."

The nickname was apropos, though Bela Lugosi had more empathy. I had made admirable progress with the suspect. She had admitted to a motive, a very believable one. She had admitted to being in the boathouse. It was clear that she was capable of murder. If only Mimi and Eric had missed their cues and stayed inside!

Bella stood up and took Peter's cup and mine to the sink. "It's getting late, my dears, and I am recently bereaved. If you don't mind, I'd like to go to bed."

Peter ignored the hint. "Harmon did not want to exercise the option, and was adamant with Mimi after you left. Why did you bother to go to his room in order to get it?"

"Harmon was too agitated to know what he was saying," Bella said firmly. "Once the play started, nothing could be allowed to interfere. As he was inclined to repeat, 'The show must go on.' I presumed by the next day he would be more rational about the option. In the interim, I did not want it destroyed."

"You lied about it in your statement," Peter said. "You said that Harmon was the one who intended to exercise the option."

"I don't adhere to the nonsense of not speaking ill of the dead. Since Harmon was in no condition to contradict me, I decided to let him take the role of the villian."

"But that's dreadful," I said.

"Then tell yourself that I was overcome with grief." She held open the door and covered an unnecessarily broad yawn. "I do hope that doesn't cause problems with your investigation. I'd hate to miss my appointment Monday morning in Farberville."

Peter and I went back to the bench in the garden. It was becoming very familiar by now, a home away from home. The moon had risen; it was perched on the cupid's head like a whimsical wisp of a hat. From the edge of the lake, frogs croaked an atonal song of unrestrained lust. Even the crickets chirped suggestively.

The garden by moonlight, the stars glittering, the sounds of nature at its horniest. I gave myself a pinch. "Well, it was instructive. We know that Bella was there and that she later took the option. She seemed so damned genteel. I'm disappointed in her—and I hope her roses all droop."

"I'm surprised you missed the most pertinent comment."

"What-did-I-miss?" It rushed out as one indignant word.

"If Harmon wasn't planning to exercise the option, then Mimi doesn't have a motive. She must have been telling the truth about that."

"Go call that sheriff person and tell him! Without a motive, his case is a butterfly net," I said. "He might as well arrest Mrs. Robison-Dewitt. I can see it: She was skulking about in a long flannel nightgown, a croquet mallet clutched in her bony fingers. She sees movement by the boathouse and creeps over to investigate. Her nostrils flare as she smells the residual alcohol on Hamon's breath. Outraged, she flings the mallet and—"

"She has an alibi."

"Or so she says," I said, deflated. It had been amusing, if whimsical. "What's her alibi?"

"It's already been confirmed. She was playing pinochle with another of the guests until almost three o'clock in the morning. When pressed, she turned pink and sputtered that they had lost track of the time and that she was not in the habit of visiting gentlemen's bedrooms in the middle of the night."

"I don't doubt that. Who's the gentleman?"

"Policemen don't gossip—it's unprofessional. Now, if we eliminate Bella and Mrs. Robison-Dewitt, then we're left without any suspects. Sheriff Lafleur may prove reluctant for that reason to dismiss Mimi. A night in jail won't hurt her. On the contrary, she may be safer there than she would be at the Mimosa Inn."

"Safer—locked up with rapists and murderers?"

"I believe the county facitlity specializes in drunken drivers and horse thieves. Only in the big city do we have the more hardened criminals."

"County facilities are not country inns."

"Whoever murdered Harmon is probably feeling secure right now, with Mimi detained at the sheriff's office as the prime suspect. If our murderer discovers that she's been released, he is apt to get nervous."

"And kill again?" I looked at the dark shadows surrounding us on every side. Did Peter have a gun? Would Suzetta lend me hers? Could I sleep with an oar under my pillow?

"It does happen in mystery novels," Peter said. "Just as the bumbling cop points his finger in accusation, the pointee falls dead from an obsure South American ant venom. The real culprit rises from the flames like a phoenix."

"I'm pleased to know that you can read something more complex than the Sunday comics," I said, irritated by his lackadaisical attitude. "Could we please stay on the subject?"

"My apologies, Miss Marple. Did the vicar's parlor maid ever vanish from the loo within thirty seconds?"

His uncanny reference reminded my of the movie—and the two-hour period of darkness that permitted all the actors to make an astounding number of exits and entrances.

"Did you watch all of the movie?" I asked abruptly.

His teeth glinted in the moonlight. "I was sitting beside you, Claire. I thought my alibi was impeccable."

"You know perfectly well that I fell asleep. You certainly could have slithered away and returned for the final credits. Everyone else seems to have done so."

"I wish I had slithered off to the boathouse to watch the drama there, but I didn't. I watched every minute of the movie, althought I missed some of the dialogue because of a buzzing snore."

"I do not snore."

"That may require further investigation. Perhaps I could put a tape recorder next to your bed."

"You have not been invited into my bedroom."

"Not yet," he murmured. The teeth glinted briefly again.

I sternly turned my thoughts from the bedroom to the boathouse. Bella had left about ten-thirty; Mimi had arrived moments later. Eric came outside in time to see her walk toward the back of the inn. The times began to swirl around my head like the smoke from Bella's cigarette.

"Eric promised to search Harmon's room for the option and the master script," I said. "He won't find the option, obviously, but he may have had success with the script. I'm going to ask him."

Peter trailed me out of the garden. The porch swing was bereft of its courting couple, to my relief. We found Eric in the office, almost invisible behind a pile of folders and ledger books.

"I have to pay accounts Monday," he explained in a panic-stricken voice. "The lawyer called to say that he could do nothing until Mimi was formally charged. Will—will she be charged, Lieutenant?"

Peter shook his head. "I doubt it, although it is out of my jurisdiction. Claire has proved that Mimi did not have a motive. I'll call Sherff Lafleur in the morning and see what I can do."

"Thank God. I didn't know what to do if . . . ."

"Pay the accounts so that the Mimosa Inn will be here when Mimi returns," I inserted tartly, hoping to jog him out of despair. "Did you search the room?"

"Yes. I couldn't find the option, but the other thing is here somewhere. Maybe it's under this . . . well, I may have put it in a file . . . no, here it is!" He produced a thin stack of papers clipped together.

Resisting the urge to rip the script out of his hand, I accepted it with a grateful smile. "Thanks, Eric. Everyone talked about it, but no one actually saw it."

Peter made a rumbling noise behind me. I grasped the script tightly to my chest and tried to scoot around him. "Good night," I trilled optimistically.

"The script?" he said, holding out his hand.

"I had it first. You can read it in the morning."

When the dust settled, I had agreed to share the master script if he would share the official statements. We switched on a lamp in the drawing room and read in silence. A peeping Tom could have mistaken us for an old married couple, both parties too bored for anything risqué.

Peter had already read the statements; he was gazing at me when I finished the last of them. "Well, Miss Marple?"

"I have to ask Eric something," I said. I went into the office and returned shortly thereafter. "Now I have to ask Mimi a question. Do cells have telephones?"

"I doubt it," Peter said, clearly mystified by my secretive expression. "Visiting hours are usually from four to six—and that's in the afternoon, not the middle of the night."

"I think I know what happened, but I have to talk to Mimi. If you won't convince Sheriff Lafleur to cooperate, I'll climb the wall and whisper through the bars." I tried for a coldly determined stare, as though I could will him into compliance.

"The sheriff will not be pleased at your request. Why can't it wait until morning, Claire?"

"What kind of humanitarian are you? Poor Mimi is sobbing on a cot in a filthy cell, no doubt convinced that she'll end up in prison—or worse! Eric is liable to collapse, taking the Mimosa Inn with him!" I realized I was a bit loud, and dropped my voice to a whisper. "If you'll do this tiny favor, I'll tell you who murdered Harmon Crundall."

"Do you know?"

"I have a fairly good idea, yes. And I think I know how it was done, and for what reason." I twitched my foot impatiently. "But I cannot explain until I talk to Mimi."

"Mimi is asleep. Sheriff Lafleur is asleep, and will not appreciate being roused by idle speculation. Tell me your theory and let me decide what needs to be done."

"I have qualms about a slander suit. Are you going to help or not, Peter? I'd appreciate it, but I can handle it alone if necessary." The perfect picture of a self-sufficient woman, who had no idea where the county jail was, or how high the walls and thick the bars. Or any experience with ropes and pitons, which always made me think of Armenian bread.

After a prolonged sigh, Peter said, "It'll take some diplomacy to get us in. I'll use the office telephone."

I sent Eric upstairs to fetch clean clothes for Mimi. Peter called everyone except the governor, then told me that we would be permitted a short conversation with Mimi. I suspected from his black expression that he would be unhappy with anything less than a murderer tied up in a pink ribbon. Within the hour.

It took almost half an hour of grim silence to drive to the county jail, an unpretentious brick building under a yellowish streetlight. A sleepy-eyed deputy checked Peter's identity at the door, looked at me as if I deserved a cell of my own, and finally led us down a hallway to a metal door.

Mimi leapt to her feet as the door opened, bewilderment flooding her face. "Claire? Peter? What are you doing here? Did something happen to Eric?"

"No, he's worried about you, but he's holding up as well as can be expected. He sent a change of clothes for you." I turned to Peter. "Are you going to wait outside the cell or in the car?"

"In the car." He gave me an ominous look before he stomped down the hall and out of sight.

Hoping the car would be there when I came out, I shut the door. "I want you to tell me exactly what you did Friday night, from the dinner nonsense until you went to bed. Don't ask questions; just talk."

Mimi sat down on the bed and cupped her face in her hands. "I've been over it a thousand times in the last eight hours. I don't see what good it will do to—"

"Begin with dinner," I suggested.

"Okay, but it won't get. me out of here. Harmon pretended to pass out at about nine. Suzetta and I helped him upstairs, then I slipped down the back stairs to make sure the dessert trays were ready. It's not easy to play a role with twenty hungry guests below."

"I'll keep that in mind," I said, impatient to hear what I anticipated.

"Suzetta waited in Harmon's room until I returned, then we went to the middle of the stairs to have the argument. I went back to Harmon's room to lure him out of the bedroom for a rendezvous, and—"

"You didn't have to follow the dialogue, though," I said. "You both already knew what was going to happen and the audience was downstairs at dinner."

"True. It was more a matter of being in the right spot so that any stray guest could collect the clue. I did have a quick drink so that my lipstick would be on the glass, but we just—chatted."

"What did you talk about?"

"Harmon was delighted with the production, but he seemed worried that something might interfere and ruin 'the show.' I assured him that all was well and offered to sneak up a dinner tray. He said he would eat when he reached his house; I said that I would see him at the boathouse at ten-thirty. I left." She shrugged.

"In your statement, you said that you reached the boathouse at ten-thirty, as scheduled. Did you see anyone else on the way there or the way back?"

She curled her legs under her and gave me a pensive look. "No, I wish I had, but I didn't. When I left, Eric was supposed to be outside, but he must have been a minute or two late. He can do calculations to the third decimal point in his head, but he's not too good with time. I presumed that he had been delayed by something."

"Did you tell the sheriff?"

"That my husband can't tell time? No, Claire, I didn't . . . What's going to happen to me? Will I be—"

"No questions," I interrupted. I thought I heard the

sound of a car engine being started in the distance. Surely he wouldn't. "What did Harmon say in the boathouse?"

"Out of the blue he said something about the option expiring at midnight Monday and not to worry," Mimi said with another shrug. "Then he said that Monday was going to bring a few surprises, but he refused to elaborate. He made a joke about it being time for his murder—" She broke off, blinking furiously to hold back the tears. "I didn't kill Harmon, Claire—you've got to believe me!"

I stood up and pounded on the cell door to bring the jailer. "I know you didn't, Mimi. Peter will arrange for your release in the morning so that you can attend my production of 'The Murder at the Mimosa Inn.' Ten o'clock, in the drawing room."

"You know who . . . ?"

I pounded again. "I hope so. Try to get some sleep, and I'll see you tomorrow."

The deputy unlocked the door and escorted me out of the jail. The car was there, complete with surly driver. His resentment faded as I explained my theory, and by the time we parked in the stable, half an hour later, he was almost smiling.

TWELVE

Peter and I stayed up the remainder of the night, agonizing over the details of the final act. Furtive calls were made, as well as other preparations. At one point, we pulled Eric from his bed to discuss the projector, and at sunrise I pulled Caron from hers to rehearse her role. Caron's initial response cannot be reproduced without danger of editorial censorship. In essence, she is not her mother's little sunshine until the sun is fairly high in the sky.

At eight o'clock, all the guests and theater members were roused for breakfast (cheese grits and biscuits, naturally), and then herded to the drawing room and peremptorily told to wait. The staff gradually assembled in the back of the room. At nine-fifteen we were ready to raise the curtain. There was only one major flaw: Mimi and Arlo Lafleur had not yet arrived.

"Call him again," I told Peter in an undertone. "The group is not going to sit for this much longer."

"He's on his way." It was not the first time we had had this conversation. I felt like a neophyte actress preparing to go on stage, which in a sense I was. All the standard symptoms of stage fright were present, from boiling stomach to icy hands. To add to my distress, Mrs. Robison-Dewitt shuddered to a halt in front of us like a semi at a gas pump.

"What is the meaning of this?" she demanded of Peter, failing to notice me beside him. Intentionally, I surmised with a sniff.

"It will be clarified, in every sense of the word," Peter said. "Would you please return to your seat until we're ready to begin?"

"I will not, Lieutenant Rosen. Unless you have some written proof of your authority, I shall go to my room to—"

"Play pinochle?" I inserted sweetly. I will admit to a small, suggestive wink.

"Well! I never in all my—how can you permit this outrageous—I shall speak to my attorney!" Mrs. Robison-Dewitt stalked back to her seat and sat down in a haze of noxious fumes.

Peter winced. "Officially, you never saw those statements, Claire. She's likely to call the Justice Department to report the infringement of her constitutional rights."

The back door opened in the midst of his lecture. A wan Mimi came in, followed by a frigid Lafleur and his posse. Eric rushed Mimi into the office for a private welcome, while Peter advanced warily to deal with the sheriff.

"I hope you know what you're doing, Rosen," Lafleur said, including me in his tight frown. His mouth reminded me of a bunny's posterior, but at least his bifocals worked properly.

"So do I," Peter said. "I respect your misgivings about this, and I want you to know I appreciate your cooperation, reluctant or not. It's almost nine-thirty. Shall we begin?"

The audience muttered as Peter and I went to the front of the room. I looked around to confirm that all the players were present. Bruce stood in the back of the room, arms folded and expression cold. He was, I suspected, worried about whatever revelations I had in mind. In the back row, Nickie twisted his mustache between his thumb and first finger. He, too, was worried.

Bella Crundall was not. From one corner she gave me a coy little wave. She wore the same blue suit and white gloves she had worn the previous morning, and the jaunty little hat. The grieving widow had enjoyed a restful night of sleep.

Suzetta sat on the edge of a chintz armchair. Her hair was restrained in a bun on her neck, and she wore a severe dark dress and matching glasses. The giddy harem girl was forever gone; in her place, we had a sober business major.

My darling daughter was draped like a plastic protector across a second armchair. She flicked out her tongue with reptilian disdain, then sank further into the fabric. Later, I promised myself, I would suggest a certain refinement of her drawing room manner.

Mimi and Eric came out of the office, glowing foolishly. The sheriff and his deputies took positions near the exits. We were all present, and the show at last could go on.

Peter waited until the mutters faded. "I apologize for any inconvenience this gathering may have caused, but I know that we all hope to be allowed to leave as soon as possible. For that reason, I have asked Mrs. Malloy to assist me in a little experiment."

Grumbles of skepticism followed. Clinching the podium, I resisted an urge to curtsy and exit stage left as quickly as possible. The whole thing seemed sillier by the second.

Peter looked at his watch, then continued. "We are going to reconstruct the events that took place Friday night. If you will cooperate, I think we may be able to discover the identity of the murderer, who is in this room—now."

The grumbles peaked in a wave that threatened to wash us out the window. Mrs. Robison-Dewitt stirred indecisively, remembered my pinochle comment, and settled for an equine snort. The other guests reacted with varying degrees of disbelief and alarm, while the policemen watched impassively, as though accustomed to daily doses of melodramatic dénouements.

"It is now nine-thirty, so we'll have to take a few liberties with the schedule," Peter said. "Friday night all of us were in the dining room. Will you please take the same seats? We'll roll the clock back to the moment when the script took an interesting twist. I will play the role of Harmon Crundall."

On that macabre note, we trooped into the dining room, bustled about, and finally sat down at the tables as requested. Mimi and Eric stood in the doorway to the kitchen. Dr. Chong Li announced that he was drinking coffee at that exact moment Friday night, and Peter smilingly sent the busboy into the kitchen. Once the coffee was poured, Peter congratulated us on our keen recollection of the previous seating arrangement, then beckoned to Suzetta, who had taken her seat across from me.

"I believe we're to make a grand entrance," he said. "I'm not talented enough to dive into a plate of food, but I would like to go through the motions."

Suzetta stood up and joined him. The room was silent as they weaved to out table, sat down, and pretended to read menus. I wondered if Peter was adding a bit more zest to the role than necessary; his eyes were rolling and his body swaying like a metronome.

"Mrs. Crundall, your turn for a grand entrance!" he called. He took a drink of water and let it dribble down his chin. A ham of great magnitude, my policeman.

Bella appeared in the doorway. "I fail to see the point of his charade, Lieutenant Rosen. It brings back painful memories, and I therefore refuse to participate."

"Perfectly understandable. Claire will be delighted to save you any discomfort." He flopped a hand at me.

We had discussed it earlier, and although I was not

precisely delighted, I was prepared. I went to the door, turned around, and took Bella's earlier path to the table.

"I'm afraid I don't know my lines."

Peter sobered up. "That's all right. Now, at this time Mrs. Crundall returned to her bungalow. Shortly thereafter, Harmon fell into the potatoes and Suzetta and Mimi carried him upstairs. The rest of the guests went to the porch for a brandy while the chairs were moved and the projector brought in. If you please . . . ?"

Like spooked cattle, the guests stampeded for the safety of the porch. I lingered to watch Suzetta and Mimi pretend to help Peter upstairs, then went to the porch and took my position by the window.

Bruce leaned against the railing beside me. "It's rather early for these people to want drinks. Am I required to drag out the bar in the name of dramatic integrity?"

"No, it can stay in the closet, as far as I'm concerned."

He gazed steadily at me for a moment, then nodded and moved away. I looked through the window in time to see Suzetta and Mimi stage their argument in the middle of the stairs, while Peter listened from the top. When they finished, he sent Mimi upstairs. Suzetta started for the door, but he caught her arm.

"You're forgetting something, Suzetta. Didn't you speak to Nickie Merrick before announcing that the movie would begin soon?"

"Did I?" She wrinkled her nose. Adorably.

Without moving, Peter raised his voice. "Merrick, I believe you and Suzetta met in the drawing room at this point."

"It wasn't anything of significance," Nickie protested in a sulky voice. "It wasn't in the script."

"Is that so?" Peter said with a show of amazement. "Well, it was one of the events preceding the movie, so we'd best include it. Try to recall the exact words, please."

Nickie jerked his mustache as he went into the drawing

room. As the rest of us gaped from the porch, he took Suzetta's arm and loudly said, "We're a minute or so behind on the script. Get everyone inside for the movie."

"Okay." She opened the door and added, "Time for the movie. I just love movies, don't you." Her voice was flat and cold, a total opposite of her Friday night trill.

"Very good." Peter beamed at them, then at us. "The chairs are arranged as they were before. It is important that everyone choose the same seat for the movie."

"Surely we are not expected to sit through a second viewing of the movie," Mrs. Robison-Dewitt said. Several others nodded in support.

"This is a homicide investigation," Peter said, abruptly the steely professional. "I presume that everyone concerned is eager to assist. Now, sit down."

She and her groupies sat down. Peter made a production of checking the time, then said, "It is now ten o'clock. The deputies will close the curtains, although of course we will not be able to achieve the level of darkness we had Friday night. Any of you who left the room must repeat the actions as accurately as possible. Eric, the movie."

Gossamer figures moved across the screen as the music began. Peter stared at his watch for almost fifteen minutes, then said, "At this point, Harmon Crundall went down the back stairs to meet Mimi in the boathouse. Suzetta went upstairs to search his room for the option, and Mimi slipped through the dining room door. When Bruce innocently followed her, he was sent to the bungalow to ask if Mrs. Crundall might want a dinner tray."

"I never went to the bungalow," Bruce said. Although his words were directed to Peter, his eyes were on me. "I stayed in the kitchen to talk to the busboys."

"Then you strayed from the script?"

"That's right—I strayed from the script. I made up the bit about hearing Bella in the bungalow."

"I wondered about that," Peter said. Whistling, he

strolled out the door to go to the boathouse. Suzetta stared after him, and with obvious reluctance rose and went upstairs as directed. Mimi and Bruce vanished into the dining room.

Bella Crundall stayed in a shadowy corner, her jaunty hat now tilted to one side. A wisp of her hair dangled across her forehead. "I refuse to participate," she repeated.

"I quite understand," I said. "I'll continue for you."

I didn't have the nerve to whistle, so I settled for a hum as I crossed the porch and went down the steps to the lawn. I went into the boathouse. "What do"—*sneeze!*—"you think?"

"It's flimsy, but we can't stop now. We'll have to pray that your scheme works and our culprit cracks. If not, I may have to take that job as a gypsy fortune-teller. Do you have any gold earrings?"

I made a face, told him that he was being pigheaded about the option, sneezed, and exited. I ducked behind a shrub to watch Mimi go into the boathouse. So far, so good, I told myself as I went through the kitchen, up the back stairs, and along the corridor to the bedroom that had once been Harmon's sty.

Suzetta looked up from an armchair, a magazine opened in her lap. "What are you doing here?" she demanded crossly.

"I'm Bella Crundall, and I'm supposed to search for the option and take it away before you have a chance to burn it." I picked up a blank piece of paper, waved it, and dashed out of the room and back downstairs to the drawing room.

On the screen, ghosts continued to flit about. The audience watched me, however, and with no amusement. I checked my watch. "Okay, Nickie leaves to meet someone." I ignored his protest and pushed him out the door. When he was outside, I added, "According to an amended statement, Bella went upstairs and then returned to her bungalow through the woods behind the stable. She did so to avoid being seen by the actors in the boathouse. Eric, it's ten-thirty-five. Aren't you supposed to be on the porch?"

He blinked. "I am, but Friday night Mrs. Robison-Dewitt stopped me at the door. I managed to put her off, but it took a minute."

I motioned to the woman. "Let's run through it, and quickly, please. We must keep to the schedule."

Mrs. Robison-Dewitt joined Eric. "Whatever I said was unimportant. It was, I believe, some comment about a clue."

Eric had told me that she had offered a substantial bit of free publicity in exchange for a hint, but I let it go and said, "Did you glance at the screen as you took your seat, Mrs. Robison-Dewitt?"

"Yes, the manservant dropped a tray and made a dreadful clatter upon seeing a corpse on a lower berth. The china was simply destroyed. It reminded me of the difficulty of finding adequate help these days."

We all stared at the screen. The china was still intact; the body undiscovered. At last, when we were all nearing hyperventilation, the corpse was exposed in a flurry of shards.

I shoved Eric onto the porch. "What do you see?"

"Mimi, going around the corner of the house," he said in a strangled voice.

"No, you don't," Mimi said from the doorway of the dining room. We all spun around to stare at her. She smiled modestly and said, "I was already upstairs, waiting for Suzetta to let me know if she found the option. I've been there for nearly five minutes."

Peter jogged across the lawn and bounded onto the porch. "That's correct," he panted. "She left the boathouse while you were delayed by Mrs. Robison-Dewitt."

"But I saw her . . ." Eric began.

"It was dark outside, and you fully expected to see your wife. According to the script, she was there; you had no cause to doubt your subconscious premise. You saw a black-haired woman in a dark raincoat. It wasn't Mimi."

"Who was it?"

Playing the scene for maximum impact, Peter paused for a full thirty seconds. "This morning Eric saw Caron Malloy, who graciously agreed to reproduce the actions of one of the community theater members. She, like her model, had a black scarf tied around her head to resemble long, black hair."

"Friday night," I said, determined to get a glimmer of the limelight, "you saw Harmon Crundall's murderer—Suzetta Price."

From the top of the stairs came a tiny squeak. Suzetta gripped the bannister with white fingers as she looked down at us, and her glasses failed to hide the fury in her eyes.

"This is absurd. Lieutenant Rosen, are you going to permit this amateur busybody to make wild accusations about me? I happen to be on assignment—for you."

Peter gave me a perplexed frown. "Do you have any evidence to substantiate your accusation, Claire?"

"In my role of Bella Crundall, I went upstairs to find the option and secure it. Suzetta was in Harmon's room." I pointed at Bella, who hovered in her corner. "Was Suzetta there Friday night?"

"No," Bella said, "the room was empty. It was simple to take the option from the dresser and replace it with a blank from Harmon's briefcase. I did not see Suzetta."

"I may have been a minute or two late," Suzetta said. "That doesn't prove anything. You ought to arrest this woman to put her out of her self-inflicted misery."

I flashed my fangs and turned to point at Nickie Merrick. "You went outside to meet Suzetta, didn't you? You made the appointment just before the movie. Harmon's little barb at dinner alerted you to the fact that he knew about the drug transactions taking place at his beloved theater. You had to warn Suzetta to stay away from you until you could do something about Peter's presence and Harmon's tacit threat to call the police Monday morning."

"I—I think Harmon overheard me when I stopped by Suzetta's room to tell her about Rosen. His room adjoined hers, but I couldn't worry about that. I had to warn her." Nickie gave me a sad smile. "I tried to tell her Friday, but when I went to our emergency meeting places, you were there—at the boathouse, in the garden."

"Sorry, Nickie," I said truthfully.

The mustache was given a particularly vicious yank. It came off in his fingers. He stared at the tuft of black hairs, then carefully placed it in his coat pocket and said, "I told Suzetta to meet me at ten-forty-five. She never came."

"Am I accused of dealing drugs?" Suzetta squealed. It was not in the least adorable. "I am working for the police!"

"So you are," I murmured.

Caron was standing quietly by the back door, looking as if she had dipped her hair in ink. I gestured for her to join me.

"My daughter," I said, "did not attend the movie Friday night; she chose instead to remain in the bedroom to talk on the telephone. In the midst of her conversation, she noticed several things that she did not realize were important."

I could see that Caron was deciding how to best play the scene. Clenching my teeth, I hissed at her to get on with it.

"Well," she said, opting for becoming modesty, "I happened to look out the window just as a blond head started for the boathouse. It was too silly to think about, so I didn't pay any attention. But a minute later I heard someone come up the back stairs and tiptoe down the hall. I was worried it might be Mother, who doesn't understand the postpubescent psychological need for peer communication."

"So you took a quick peek?" Peter said before she could warm up to the subject.

"I saw Suzetta go into Mr. Crundall's room, wearing a raincoat. She came out a minute later with a paper in her hand and went into the Vanderhans' room. I don't know what happened to the raincoat, but she wasn't wearing it anymore."

"Did you hear anything as Suzetta went into the Vanderhans' bedroom?" he prodded.

"I heard Mrs. Vanderhan say something, then they closed the door." A humble smile on her face, Caron pulled off the scarf and stepped forward to accept an Oscar.

Peter moved in front of her. "Mimi was upstairs waiting for a report when the murder took place. Suzetta, however, decided she could deal with Harmon Crundall and still make it to the Vanderhans' room without anyone noticing the time discrepancy. To her perplexity, the original option had been removed by Bella. Had Suzetta not taken liberties with her script, she would have arrived in Harmon's room first and been able to burn the option. Suzetta was the last visitor to see Harmon alive, and she murdered him."

"You haven't proved it!" she said. Her sneer wobbled, but she recovered and tossed her chin.

I wrinkled my nose adorably. "Your bikini was drying in the bathroom last night. When could you have found time for a swim except in the middle of the night? Who could have guessed you're Olympic material?"

Peter's nose was rather adorable, too. "Since you knew Bruce was waiting on the road for Harmon, you had only one option—to take the most direct route from the other side of the lake."

"And I did sneeze at your raincoat," I added with an adorable blush. "Mold from the boathouse, you know."

"You're all crazy!"

Deputies edged forward. Nickie was pulled aside, and his sputters cut off by the click of handcuffs. Suzetta whirled around and made a dash for the door. It ended with a dent in Sheriff Lafleur's badge, nose level.

The curtain fell not on thunderous applause, but on a squeak. It was followed by a stunned silence.

T H I R T E E N

"**D**id Sheriff Lafleur find the croquet mallets?" I asked Peter.

"Eric tossed one under the porch when he came back to the drawing room. Suzetta intended to hide the other in the woods, but she never had a chance to slip away." He looked up at the waiter and gave our order, then said, "There was no question that Suzetta's was the weapon; the blood type matched and there were a few hairs and bits of flesh."

The waiter blanched. When he found his voice, it reminded me of a tree frog I once knew at the Mimosa Inn. "Would you care to see the wine list, sir?"

Peter selected a bottle of wine and allowed the waiter to flee to the kitchen. "We found the mallet in the trunk of her car, along with a black scarf and enough drugs to prove she was the campus distributor. Merrick was eager to tell us all the details of her involvement, no doubt thinking it would endear him to us."

"Did it?"

Peter discovered something of great interest on the ceiling. "We were not thrilled by any of it. Suzetta was not a regular member of the CID—thank God—but merely a civilian recruit. Last fall she was picked up with a purseful of pills, and we decided to drop the charges if she agreed to work for us. An unfortunate decision."

"Was she working for Nickie from the beginning?"

"When we first picked her up, we erroneously assumed she was a customer, not a retailer. She turned in very precise weekly reports about Merrick's movements at the theater, but she could not pinpoint the identity of the contact. Now I know why."

"Did you give her the gun?" I asked as a shiver raced up my back. "She wasn't playing when she forced me downstairs. If you hadn't popped out of the office, I wouldn't have been around to interfere with any more investigations."

"We issued a temporary permit. She convinced us that she needed it for her own safety, because of the unsavory people involved. One of them happened to be our under-cover agent."

"She strung you along for eight months?" I said with mock bewilderment. "The keen minds at the CID never suspected that their very own agent was also their drug dealer?"

"And our murderer," Peter sighed. "You did well, Claire."

"We were lucky that she believed Caron's story about the raincoat. The child did well too; I almost believed her myself."

"You've reared an accomplished liar."

I nodded graciously. The waiter sidled up to the table, a wine bottle clutched in his hand. The label was read and the cork ceremoniously examined. Then, his hand trembling so wildly that wine splashed onto the tablecloth, the waiter poured an inch into Peter's glass and stepped back to stare at us.

"Fine," Peter said after a sip. As the waiter filled my glass, he lifted his and said, "To murder."

Purple rain spewed onto the tablecloth.

"Which one?" I replied sweetly.

The waiter's eyes widened. He crammed the bottle into a bucket of ice, gurgled, and again fled to the kitchen, perhaps to find a butcher knife in case of an attack.

"The mock one, I think," Peter said. We clinked glasses across the table. "Did any of the cryptic clues escape your cunning mind?"

"Not exactly," I said, crossing my fingers in my lap. "The one that read, 'Tues. a hobo collapsed' was obviously an anagram for the boathouse, which was to be the scene of the crime. 'Do we have to pay?' was a reference to the blond wig and the synthetic hairs found there. 'An abbreviated problem of personal identity' told me that Suzetta was a P.I.—a private detective. I realized that she had to be working for the Vanderhans."

"Well done, Miss Marple. Of course, the 'batter dipped portion of minced meat, sans time limits' meant that we were looking for a croquette with a *t* and an *e*, which are the outside letters of the word 'time.' A croquet mallet was the weapon."

"What else could it be?" I murmured. "It did seem unfair that the clue was in my menu only. How did you know about that clue, Peter?"

"It was in all the menus, but you were the only one to choke on it. How did you do with the Baggies of evidence—did you deduce the significance of all of them?"

"Except one," I admitted. Candor cleanses the soul, as long as one doesn't get carried away with it. "What about you?"

"The lipstick smudge on the glass from Harmon's room indicated that a woman had been with him. Suzetta's lipstick was too dark, so it must have been Mimi's. The ashes were from the option, as we all knew, and the hairs from the wig. Is that all?"

"The mud clump, which came from Bella's shoe rather than Eric's," I said. "Did the lab report show traces of lime?"

"I received the analysis this morning, and yes, lime was present. Our forensics man raises roses himself, and he was quite excited with his findings. I didn't have the heart to tell him he was two weeks late with the monumental discovery."

"Poor, inept Eric was scripted to overhear Mimi's conversation with Harmon when the tryst was made. He said afterwards that he was opposed to the mock murder from the beginning, since he realized he was apt to bungle his role. He's going to teach incomprehensible things at Farber College next fall, and let Mimi and Bruce handle the innkeeping and theater productions. They're sticking to comedies from now on, but not the sort that take place in the Mimosa Inn's drawing room."

"Then Harmony Hills will not mar the view?"

"No," I said. "Bella tried to convince herself that Mimi had murdered her husband in order to justify exercising the option. Since she would be avenging his death, to the tune of several hundred thousand dollars, she tried very hard to believe it. Later, she felt guilty enough to allow the Vanderhans to purchase the option from her. She'll have to order her tulips from Holland."

The waiter came to the table with our order, his face carefully set in a deferential mask. We received our plates in record time, and he was again allowed to take sanctuary in the kitchen. By this time, the chef and several assistants were watching from the doorway, and the other waiters made wide circles around our table, as if we were surrounded by a haze of plague germs. I rather appreciated the privacy.

"Bella did retire," I added to Peter as I picked up my fork. "A great relief to her chemistry students."

"We forgot the final clue in the boathouse—the book of matches with two missing from the left side. Is that the one you could not decipher?"

"Nobody was left-handed," I said. "I watched Bella when she lit a cigarette. The only other person who smoked was Eric, and he was most definitely right-handed."

"But he often turns the matchbook upside down."

"Feeble at best," I sniffed. I gave all of my attention to the food, hoping that the recapitulation was over. One clue remained, the one that read, "The rickety building holds the answer." Caron, who knew what it meant, had refused to discuss it until she had communicated with every peer in Farberville about her vital role in the solution of the murder. She has a lot of peers, although not one of them can equal her melodramatic flair.

I finally put down my fork. "Better than crow à la king and humble pie," I said with a grin.

"That depends on who's cooking." His grin was broader, but he'd had more practice. "Did you read this month's copy of the *Ozark Chronicle*? Not only did I fail to make the cover, I wasn't even mentioned. It hurt my feelings; I thought Mrs. Robison-Dewitt and I were friends."

"Pinochle!"

The waiter had unobtrusively wormed his way to the table to remove our plates. At my outburst, he gave a shriek, dropped his tray, and dashed for the kitchen. I wondered if coffee was out of the question.

"She was playing with Dr. Chong Li," Peter said, "but don't repeat it to anyone—ever. The gentleman lost seventeen dollars and forty-five cents."

"A closet gambler," I said. "The woman deserves to have her vice exposed to the world. However, as long as I never see her again, I suppose I can be magnanimous. Shall we go?"

Peter slapped his forehead. "We forgot one of the cryptic clues," he said in a display of dismay. "I'll try to catch the waiter's eye to get a check while you expound."

Damn. Time for a devious ploy. "Aren't you going to lecture me about interfering with a police investigation? It tends to be our standard parting conversation."

"No, in your role of amateur busybody you were of great assistance to the Farberville CID—this time. The clue?"

"Did we forget one? I thought we . . ." I faded as I took in his knowing smile. "Well, what was it?"

"I believe it said, 'The rickety—'"

"I know what it said. What does it mean?"

"The letters *e-r-i-c* are hidden in the first two words of the clue, which of course exposes the identity of the mock murderer: Eric. He stopped on the porch to put on a wig. That's when he saw Suzetta leave the boathouse, which led to all the confusion."

"Some of it, anyway," I said, thinking of the confusion that had arisen from a certain log in a cove. It was, I decided, time to resolve the problem once and for all. An investigation was necessary, even if it lasted all night.

I curled a finger at our waiter, who was slumped in a chair next to the kitchen door, fanning himself with a menu.

"Check, please," I called. It was the least I could do.